THE MAGIC

Mystical Realms 1

McKinlay Thomson

MENAGE AMOUR

Siren Publishing, Inc.
www.SirenPublishing.com

A SIREN PUBLISHING BOOK
IMPRINT: Ménage Amour

THE MAGIC OF YOU
Copyright © 2014 by McKinlay Thomson

ISBN: 978-1-62741-517-0

First Printing: July 2014

Cover design by Harris Channing
All art and logo copyright © 2014 by Siren Publishing, Inc.

PUBLISHER
Siren Publishing, Inc.
www.SirenPublishing.com

DEDICATION

To my husband Grant. For always loving me and supporting me in everything I do.

THE MAGIC OF YOU

Mystical Realms 1

MCKINLAY THOMSON
Copyright © 2014

Chapter One

"One more hour and you're on holiday."

Jessica Whittemore looked up from her latest candle display, when her part-timer Elise spoke. She was almost finished for the day and then she could run upstairs and pack.

Jessica lived in a small flat above the occult shop she owned and ran. Mystical Thistles was a small store tucked in a little laneway in Notting Hill. Jessica sold all things magical, from candles and gemstones to spells, books, costumes and tarot cards. She had potions and lotions and even sold statues of dragons and witches on broomsticks.

"Maybe I shouldn't go. I've got Merlin to look after and I feel like I'm dumping my responsibilities on you," Jessica said. She continued to fiddle with the display. Something wasn't right and it looked odd, but she couldn't put her finger on what it was missing.

"Don't be silly." Elise told her. "I can handle the extra hours. I need the money. Besides, you have had this trip booked for weeks and you have already paid, and Merlin will be fine by himself for a while. It will be no hassle to run upstairs and feed him before I go. He spends most of his time running around the shop anyway."

Merlin was Jessica's jet-black house cat. He was spoilt and chubby and Jessica would miss him. Elise was right. She really needed this holiday. She hadn't been on one since she opened the shop three years before.

"You're right," She replied. "It's going to be great. Three whole weeks to myself, exploring the mystical wonders of England."

"As much as you need this holiday, choosing to go on a tour of 'magical England' isn't my idea of fun. You could be lying on a beach somewhere warm, somewhere tropical. Instead you're going to be running around on a bus, with a bunch of crazy people."

"Hey, I'm one of those crazy people and so are you for that matter. Remember where you work."

"Yes, but there is a difference between being pagan and gallivanting around the countryside hunting for magic."

"It more than just that. We are going to some of the most magical spots in the whole country. Tell me there isn't anything magical about Stonehenge. And we are going to a little pub in Snitterfield that was supposed to be run by goblins and frequented by all sorts of magical creatures."

"I would rather go on the *Harry Potter* tour of London. At least then it's over in one day and you could hit the beach."

Jessica sighed and went back to her candles. Elise would never understand the pull she had to any place magical. It was why she had chosen this particular store for her shop. She could feel its magical pull and knew from the moment that she saw it that it was the place for her.

Jessica had always felt a magical connection to things and places. It was like their magic called to her. It was more than just playing around to Jessica. She had a magic ability, but she very rarely told people.

How do you tell someone that you had the power to pull sickness and disease from their body and into yours? But it was more than that. She could do it for all sorts of things, like the effect of drugs on a person's body. All Jessica had to do was place her hands on the person's skin and open her mind and pull the sickness from their body and into hers. Then she could expel it from her body before it had time to take hold of her.

It was hard on her body and usually left her weak for days afterward. Jessica knew her power was special and if people found out what she could do she would be used and abused for it. It was the main reason she didn't tell people.

There was this one incident when Jessica was shopping for groceries. This little boy, no more than six, was shopping with his mother. All of a sudden he had curled up in a ball on the floor, complaining that his stomach hurt. The child was racked with pain and the mother was frantic. Jessica couldn't leave him like that. She quickly approached the boy and lifted his top. Placing her hands on his stomach, she drew the sickness from his body into hers.

Once she found the boy was all right, Jessica had rushed from the store and fled to her flat. It had taken her hours to rid her body of the illness and it had taken over a week to get her strength back. It had turned out to be appendicitis.

Jessica knew she had saved the boy's life that day, but she had never gone back to that grocery store. She didn't want people to ask questions and thought it best to just stay away and shop someplace else.

Jessica never regretted helping the people she could and often wished she were able to help more. But she had to think about her own well-being as well. She wasn't sure of the long-term effects that this magic would have on her body.

There was no way you could tell Jessica was different just from looking at her. She was average height and slim. Most people would say she was petite. Her curly blonde hair fell to her shoulders and when she wore it up in a ponytail it would fan out and bounce when she walked. She had blue eyes and a spattering of freckles on her nose and cheeks.

She moved away from the candle display, giving up. It was a lost cause. Elise could fix it later. For the remainder of the hour, she potted around the shop, moving things back to their proper place. As soon as the clock hit the hour, she turned the open sign to "Closed" and then locked the door.

Elise said good-bye and left by the back door. Jessica locked it behind her and then, grabbing the money from the till, went upstairs to finish the accounts.

* * * *

Jessica exited the bus in Snitterfield and flung her purse over her shoulder. Two weeks into her trip and she was having a blast. They had left London and headed south where they had stopped in Brighton. They had stood on the beach at midnight, naked, and chanted. She wasn't shy about running around naked with a bunch of strangers. It was dark and most of the people on the tour were female.

On the bus, Jessica had met a lovely couple that was newly married. Samantha and Dale were taking the "Magical England" tour, despite the fact they thought it was just hocus-pocus, because it offered the best rate to tour the country. They didn't mind that they had to stop at places that held magical significance if it saved them some money. They were conveniently missing for the chant.

Once they had left Brighton they had headed to Portsmouth and an old sailing ship that was said to be magical because it was the only surviving ship of a storm that had taken out twelve others. Jessica got no readings on her inbuilt magical radar, so she thought that it was a load of baloney.

After that they had gone up to Stonehenge. It was really a magical place and Jessica loved every second that they had spent there. She stood in the middle and let the currents wash over her.

Jessica would have loved to come back there at night and do it naked. It was such a sensual feeling, leaving her feeling turned on and in need. Luckily she had packed her battery-operated boyfriend, so she had gone back to her room and taken care of her need. Whoever had built Stonehenge was well-versed in sensual magic.

She didn't think anyone else had got the same readings she did. When she went down to dinner and had mentioned it to the others, they had looked at her like she had lost the plot.

Now they were finally at the funny little pub she had been waiting to visit. It looked like your average country pub. It was a white double-story building with a slate roof and a vine growing up the brick chimney. Jessica pulled open the door and entered the main bar.

She didn't get any magical vibes, and when she looked around the dark interior she didn't see any stand-out magical creatures either. She walked over and took a seat at the wooden bar. It was stained a dark color that matched the low ceiling beams. A large inglenook sat on the opposite wall and the roaring fire kept away the chilly English air.

Jessica turned to the tall, non-goblin-looking barman and ordered a beer. She wasn't normally a drinker, but thought that she should at least have one. Whilst in Rome and all that. Taking a sip, she scrunched up her nose at the bitter taste. The ale was dark and didn't taste any better on the second sip. She placed it down on the bar and looked around.

The place was empty this early in the evening. The dinner rush was yet to start, but Jessica didn't think it would make much difference. There were a couple of older men drinking at the bar. They looked like regulars. There were also a few men in work outfits that probably just knocked off a job site and were having a knock off before heading home. It was different from the hustle and bustle of Notting Hill, but Jessica could appreciate the slower pace of the countryside.

Disappointed with the lack of magic the pub contained, Jessica decided to explore the village. She wasn't hungry yet anyway and wanted to look around before it got dark. Not bothering to finish her beer, she exited the building and slowly strolled down the lane.

Her thick jeans and boots kept the cold off her legs, but the thin white peasant blouse was useless against the chilly English air. Jessica wrapped her coat around her body and tied the belt tight. She placed her hands in her pockets to keep them warm. She should have packed her gloves. Oh well, too late now. Maybe she could buy some at the general store tomorrow.

Jessica kept walking, letting her mind wander. She hoped that Elise was doing all right at the shop. She had promised not to ring her every five minutes and let Elise take the responsibility for a while, and so far she had held to the arrangement. But she still worried. It was her livelihood that she was thinking about, but it was more than that too. It was not only her shop, but her passion. She loved everything magic and always had.

Jessica stopped when she reached a little church that sat opposite a school. It was an old brick building and made her smile. She never went to church, but if she did it would be a pretty one like this. She turned away and kept walking. As she passed an old red telephone box, Jessica's inner magic radar went on high alert.

Something was pulling at her insides, telling her to keep going. Not one to shy away from the unknown, she moved down the lane. The farther away from the pub she went, the stronger the pull. It was almost like the pub had a protection spell around it. Was that why she hadn't got any magical readings from the place? Was something blocking the magic? Now that she was outside it perimeter, there was nothing to stop the magic from flowing.

She didn't know where the source of the pull was coming from, she just knew she had to follow her gut and it was taking her away from the pub and into a residential part of the village. It was almost an urgent feeling inside her now. Jessica broke out into a jog.

As she ran around a curve in the road, she began to sweat and puff. The magical pull was making her insides scream. She knew she must be close. She reached a house in the lane and stopped. This was it. This house was the source of the magic. It was a Tudor-style cottage, with a thatched roof and lead windows. An ivy vine grew wild, covering the whole left side of the cottage. A small cobblestone path led up to the front door, and a rose-covered arch stood about halfway down. Jessica's insides clawed at her, forcing her to start down the path.

She was getting nervous. Jessica didn't know what sat on the other side of that door. She didn't get any bad vibes from the magic she was sensing, but that didn't mean it wasn't masked. Black magic usually left a foul taste in her mouth, but a strong witch could mask the magic and make people think it was good.

She stood at the path, shaking with the intensity of the magical pull. This was what she had come on the trip for, to let her magical senses grow and see what magic she could find around England. So why did she hesitate?

Jessica placed one booted foot on the path and then stopped. Indecision was running rife through her body. She slowly placed the other foot onto the path and stopped once more. What the heck. In for a penny, in for a pound and all that garbage. She mustered up her courage and made her way down the path.

Jessica reached the rose-covered wooden arch and stopped once more. The magic was coming from the arch, not the house. It was pulling her to walk through. She could feel the veil of magic that ran down like a curtain. Placing her hand through the veil, Jessica felt cold wind. Something was on the other side.

It was a gateway. Jessica had read about openings into other places. Magical places where fairies and other magical creatures lived. But she thought it was just a myth, something that was passed down from generation to generation but had no basis in fact. Silly really, as she had seen and done things in the realm of magic that she couldn't explain. The existence of other worlds was something she never thought was real.

Jessica pulled her hand back. The pull was telling her to go through the veil and into the other world. Jessica wanted to, but at the same time didn't. The chance to see another realm was too great to pass up, but what if she couldn't get back and she was stuck there? Then again, would she ever get another opportunity like this? Gateways to other realms didn't pop up every day.

Taking a big breath, she held it and stepped through the curtain. Jessica felt herself spinning, and the force that pulled her through the veil made the air whoosh from her body. Her world went black and she thought she was going to pass out. Just when she thought she couldn't handle any more she was released from the veil, which sent her flying to the ground below.

She landed with a hard thump on the ground, leaving her winded and gasping for breath. She lay there until her breath returned and when she picked herself up from the ground she was light-headed and disorientated.

God, she felt like crap. She had really taken a beating. Her ribs hurt from the pressure that had squeezed her as she passed through the veil. Her back throbbed where she landed hard on the ground. She must have landed on a rock.

Jessica looked back toward the gateway. It was gone. Shit, how was she going to get home? She swiped her hands around looking for it, but felt nothing. The magical pull was gone and her internal radar sat silent once more. She was well and truly stuck.

Maybe going through the veil wasn't the best idea after all? Jessica debated about whether to stay there and see if the gateway opened again or to take a look around the new realm. She had no idea where she was. It looked like she was still in rural England, but the village was gone and all she could see for miles were fields of grass dotted with the odd tree or bush. There was no path and no buildings. There wasn't even a fence. A few boulders but nothing else. There wasn't a soul to be seen either.

Jessica stood there and turned in a circle. No matter which way she looked there was nothing. The best option would be to find a village or shelter before dark. Then she could find out where she was and how to get home again. She just had to figure out which way to go.

The sky was overcast and she couldn't see the sun. With no way to tell which way was north, she started to walk toward a large boulder in the distance. It sat on top of a small grassy knoll, and from there she thought maybe she might be able to see something that would lead her to shelter.

Jessica shook her head as she walked. She had really gotten herself in a pickle this time. Damn her inquisitive nature, and her magic. If she ever made it home, she was never leaving her shop.

Chapter Two

"Enough!" Baen roared and slammed his fist down on the table. "My decision is made."

King Baen Caladh glared at the nobles gathered at the meeting table. He was tired. Tired of war and tired of the constant fighting amongst his nobles. He turned to the leader of his army and his lover of five years.

"Send out men to scout the border. The moment King Balfour's men cross, I want to know about it. There will be no battle unless provoked."

"At once, Majesty," Carr replied. With a wave of his hand, a foot soldier rushed to do his bidding. The men were well trained and wouldn't need to be told twice.

"You may all go."

Baen sat back down and ran a frustrated hand through his hair. The nobles all quickly retreated. Carr was the only one who stayed behind. The meeting had taken place in the long hall of Baen's castle. He held all his meetings in the room. Long and narrow, it had a large table that ran its length with a dark maroon rug underneath. Tapestries hung along the walls depicting battles that had been fought and won over time. A large hearth warmed the cold stone-walled room, and two heavy wooden doors at the far end were the only way in and out.

"How am I expected to win a war when my men are fighting amongst themselves?" Baen asked.

His lover stood and approached, coming up behind his chair. As he started to massage his tense shoulders, Baen relaxed into his touch.

"The nobles grow lazy and greedy. You have managed to keep the peace with Balfour for years. It has turned them in to milksop. Now that the peace has ended, most don't want to leave the comforts of their hearths to fight." Carr was more than just a lover and the leader of his army. He was Baen's confidant and friend.

Carr was a tall, muscled man only slightly shorter than Baen's great height. His shoulder-length brown hair was scruffy on his head. Baen wouldn't call him handsome, but he had a presence that had always attracted him. He had soulful brown eyes that had small gold flecks and a scar on his face that ran from just below his left eye to his strong chin. His chest was covered with scars too. He was a warrior and had seen a lot of battle in his thirty-seven years.

Baen had seen just as much fighting. He was only older than Carr by two years and the men had grown up together. They were both sent to the same noble to learn to fight, but it wasn't until they were back at his father's castle that they had discovered their love for each other.

Baen was a giant of a man, and, even though Carr was a big man himself, he still seemed small when standing next to him. He had black hair that fell halfway down his back, and gray eyes, which Carr had often referred to as piercing.

"That slave-trading mongrel will never rule Marak. Not as long as I'm standing." Baen stood and pulled his lover to stand in front of him. Roughly grabbing Carr by the scruff of the neck, he drew him in and took his mouth. He wasn't gentle as he thrust his tongue into Carr's.

Baen had ruled the kingdom of Marak since he was a young man of twenty-two. His father was taken by fever, leaving his mother a widow. He only had a younger sister, leaving the responsibility to him. He had taken to the throne well, and now, over seven years later, he still ruled with a compassionate but iron fist.

The familiar shiver, which he got whenever he was with his lover, ran the length of his spine and ignited his passion. Baen ground his throbbing cock against Carr's as he tried to express his love for his scarred lover.

"You need to take a wife, my lover, and get an heir for our kingdom," Carr told him breathlessly between kisses. Baen touched his forehead to Carr's, but didn't let him go from his tight embrace.

"Now is not the time for talk of women. I know my obligation and when we find a woman that suits us, she shall join us in our bed." Baen replied.

"What wife would want to share you? One look at that gorgeous cock and I would be stricken from the bedchamber." Carr took hold of Baen's hard cock and stroked it through his breeches. He let out a loud moan and arched into Carr's hand.

"I will not give you up, Carr." He panted. "Not for anyone. If this woman, whom we have yet to even find, will not accept that, then she is not the one for us."

"You may have no choice."

"No! You belong to me and that is final." Baen took Carr's mouth in another brutal but passionate kiss. The love he felt for his battle-scarred warrior was strong and he would not, could not, give him up. He didn't care that he needed an heir. They would just have to find a woman that could accept the strange relationship he wanted.

Baen didn't want a wife that would only have him in her bed. He wanted one that would accept Carr as well. They would be a triad. Baen planned to marry both and they would be equally married to each other. He knew Carr liked women as well as men. They had talked about it often. They had even gone as far as bedding a woman together. They had bedded other men together too, for that matter, before things got serious.

No, they would just have to wait and find the right woman for them. She was out there somewhere, they just hadn't met her yet. In the meantime, Carr needed to be reminded that his ass belonged to Baen, now and forever.

"Remove your clothes, my love. Then turn around and place your hands flat on the table." Baen walked over to the mantel that sat over the hearth. Opening a chest, he removed a small jar and returned to Carr's side. He removed his own clothes swiftly, leaving them where they fell.

As Carr moved into position, Baen ran his hand down his lover's scarred back and over his hard mounds. He felt Carr shiver under his touch. Reaching around, he took hold of his long cock and slowly moved his fist up and down. Placing nipping kisses along his back, Baen continued to torture his lover, until he had Carr moaning and withering beneath him.

"Baen, please, I need you inside me," Carr moaned. Baen tightened his fist, squeezing the hard length. He pushed on Carr's back until his chest lay flat on the wooden surface beneath, exposing his tight puckered star to Baen's gaze.

"Be patient, lover. I'll give you what you need, but not until I'm good and ready." Baen loved to make Carr wait. He craved the power he held over this usually strong dominant man. Baen felt pre-cum leak from his cock and drip to the floor below. He grabbed the jar and started to prepare his lover.

Scooping some of the grease onto his fingers, Baen circled Carr's pink hole, before slipping a finger inside. Carr moaned again and thrust his ass up toward him. Baen slapped his left butt check with his free hand, leaving the flesh pink.

"Settle down or I'll spank your firm ass until you do. Then I'll make you wait longer for my cock, which you are craving so badly." Baen used his firm, in-charge voice, but it was an empty threat. Carr loved to have his ass spanked, so it wasn't a punishment. He was also too desperate to get inside Carr to hold off for much longer.

Baen added another finger and scissored them in and out, stretching and widening the opening. One more finger joined the others, as Carr lay panting beneath him. When he started to thrust back onto Baen's fingers once more, he knew Carr was ready. He heard a groan when he removed his fingers and watched the little hole return to its normal shape.

Lining the head of his cock up with Carr's back entry, he slowly pushed the head of his cock against the star. Once the head popped through the ring of tight muscle, Baen grabbed Carr's hips in his large hands and rammed the rest of the way inside. When he was balls deep, he froze and savored the feel of the hot, tight passage wrapped around his long length.

Baen's heart pounded in his chest and he thought he would explode from the love he felt for the warrior below him. He started to move his hips in and out, slowly driving them both mad with the pace.

Carr wiggled and moved beneath him, trying to get him to speed up. Baen chuckled at his attempt. It would be no use and he would just have to wait until Baen was ready to give him the ride he desired.

"Your ass is so hot and tight, my lover. I could stay this way all day. You feel so good."

"Please, Baen. I need. Harder, please. Fuck me harder." Baen could hear the desperation in his lover's voice. But he wasn't swayed. He kept up the slow and steady pace, grinding his cock into Carr's ass. When he reached the bottom, he slowly retreated until just the head remained. Then he repeated it over again.

"Come on, Carr. Plead for my cock. Tell me how you want it hard and hot and deep," he whispered. He was starting to sweat and pant as he tortured them both and knew that if Carr didn't say the words soon it would be too late.

"Yes, yes, Baen, please. Fuck me. Fuck me hard and quick. Oh God." That was what Baen wanted. He tightened his grip on Carr's hips and pounded his cock into his lover's tight hole.

The only noise in the long room was the slapping of flesh and the moans of the men as they fucked, bent over the meeting table. They often made love in this room. Baen took Carr in every way possible, but this was his favorite.

It wasn't long before Carr was crying out beneath him, shooting his passion onto the floor below. Baen gave two more powerful thrusts and with a mighty shout, came into his lover's waiting hole.

Baen laid his head on his lover's back, as they panted for breath. He wrapped his arms around Carr and they stayed that way until they were both shivering again, but this time from cold, not passion. Baen slipped his softened cock from his lover and, grabbing a cloth from the mantel, cleaned them both before dressing.

When they were both dressed and back to looking like the fierce warriors they were, Baen grabbed his lover and planted another kiss on his swollen lips.

"I love you, Carr. Never forget that. No matter what happens in the future, you belong to me." He placed nippy kisses along his jaw, and waited for Carr's reply. It wasn't long in coming, Baen needing to hear the words as much as say them.

"I love you too, Baen. More than you know, but I also understand that you are king and have obligations that will come before me and our love."

"Nothing could ever be so important that I would put you second. No matter what you think or feel." He kissed him one more time, before lifting his head and turning toward the door. No amount of words would get Carr over his insecurities. Baen would just have to prove with actions that Carr came first and foremost.

* * * *

Just as they reached the wooden doors to leave there was a loud knock on the other side. Carr pulled the door open and took note of the soldier that stood there.

"Well, what is it?" Carr snapped when the young soldier just stood there with a scared look on his face. He bowed low to the king, before straightening.

"Sire, I have news. I…um," he stammered.

"Spit it out, boy. I'm not one to hurt the messenger." Baen tried to reassure the young man, but he was having none of it.

"Your sister, Sire. She is missing."

"Missing? How? Where are her guards?" Carr thundered. This wasn't the first time the princess had flown the coop. She was renowned for giving her guards the slip and taking off on her horse. He knew that Baen would be worried. The royal family had enemies that would have no problem using the princess as leverage.

"Is her horse gone? How long has she been missing?" the king asked. "Have you checked the entire castle?"

"Yes, Sire. The guards have looked everywhere and are now riding out in search. Her horse is still in the stable." He bowed his head continuously as he spoke and wrung his hands. Carr was used to the younger soldiers being afraid when in their presence, but sometimes it made it hard to get things done.

"Tell them to hold. We will ride out with them," the king said and then turned to him. "When I catch up with that sister of mine, there will be hell to pay. I have a mind to marry her off. Then she will be her husband's responsibility."

"You never would, Majesty. You love her too much to take away such an important choice," Carr reminded him. The king did love his sister and had always promised her she could find her own husband. Carr thought it was because Baen would feel like a hypocrite, to love a man and then choose his sister's bed partner for her.

He followed the king out of the long hall and through the castle to the stables. He admired his lover's form as he trailed behind. The king was a giant of a man, full of hard muscle and strong lines. He was a handsome man, not in the pretty-boy sense, but in a rugged, manly way.

Carr couldn't picture himself following the rulings of another king with the same loyalty that he did with Baen. It wasn't just because they were lovers either. Baen was a good ruler and had seen their kingdom grow and prosper despite the hardships that had befallen them. Baen had led them through not just attacks from the rulers that sat either side of Marak, but through a rainy season that had seen their crops rot and die, leaving the people hungry and without a place to live, as well as the fevers that had swept through the kingdom and killed a third of their population.

Carr loved his King with everything in him and though Baen said that they would always be together, he knew that there would come a time when he would be put aside for the good of the realm. It was just a matter of time, in Carr's opinion. Baen would need an heir and that required a wife. What woman would want to have a battle-scarred warrior in her bed taking her husband's attention? She would be queen and he couldn't see any woman wanting to share her man.

Shaking his head to rid himself of his melancholy thoughts, Carr walked through the door to the stable, to find his stallion already saddled and waiting. His horse had been with him for years and, not one for fancy words, Carr had called the big black horse Black. Pulling himself onto the horse, he adjusted the reins in his hands and waited for his King.

When Baen had finished talking with the stable master, he mounted his chestnut stallion, Selinus, and they nudged their mounts forward. Once they were over the drawbridge, they both sped up until the horses were galloping across the fields. It didn't take long to catch up with the guards. They pulled the horses to a stop and Baen went over to talk with the leader of his sister's guard.

While Carr waited, he shifted uncomfortably in his saddle. His ass was still tender from the reaming he had received. He wasn't usually in the saddle so quickly after sex and his ass was paying the price.

Carr looked back toward the castle that he had called home since he was a boy. It was a great towering structure, made from large gray stone. A great wall wrapped around the outer bailey, with a large lake resting at the base of two sides. It protected the rear of the castle from attack. The empty fields on the front meant that they could see anyone approaching for miles. The keep towered in the center of the great wall, and with the drawbridge down it was bustling with activity from the daily market, which sat just outside.

A call from his lover pulled him back to the task at hand and they were soon riding away from the castle. He would hate to be in Elvinia's shoes when her brother caught up with her. The King was getting tired of her antics, having to chase after her time and again. The idea of marrying her off wasn't a bad one. Baen would just have to make sure it was to someone the princess agreed with.

Carr nudged his horse into a faster gait and caught up with his lover. It wasn't his job to protect the King, but he would give his life for the man he loved. He took his role as the leader of the king's army seriously and always tried to stay sharp and have the best-trained soldiers in the realm. So far that had proven true, with them defeating constant attacks from the neighboring kingdoms.

Marak was a wealthy kingdom. It may be small, but good luck and hard work had seen the people and the land prosper and grow. It had had its fair share of hardships as well, but the people had always pulled together. Baen wasn't afraid to get his hands dirty and that made the people of Marak respect him all the more.

It was this wealth and good fortune that had brought attention to the neighboring kingdom's leaders. But instead of an alliance that would see the kingdoms helping each other, the other leaders tried to conquer and take what wasn't theirs.

King Balfour from Barak was their latest threat, but they had managed to keep it contained so far. Barak was to Marak's east border. It was a slave-holding land that thrived on fear and terrorized its people. It had long since run out of natural resources and its people were hungry, malnourished, and poor.

In Baen's grandfather's time, Barak had discovered a precious metal, which they had mined and used for currency. It had led to some of their people being insanely rich, whilst others went poor. Marak still worked on a barter system. They traded goods and services amongst each other. That meant that everyone had food, clothes and shelter. The men looked after the women and children. Everyone was taken care off. It didn't matter whether you were old, young, married or widowed.

Hopefully the princess hadn't fallen into Barak's evil hands. That would cause King Baen to take drastic measures. Measures that he wasn't sure any of them were ready for.

Chapter Three

Jessica had been walking for hours. Her feet were sore and she was hungry. She hadn't passed a single person, not even an animal. Maybe she should stop for the night and have a break, but it was getting cold and she didn't have anything to make a fire with. Her magic didn't extend to producing fire or laser beams.

She chuckled to herself and looked round. She could be walking in circles for all she knew. Everything looked the same. Grassy knoll after grassy knoll, littered with small shrubs and the odd boulder. What the heck was she going to do? She couldn't even make her way back to the gateway if she wanted to. She didn't know where it was. She should have left a marker. Too late now!

What was magical about this realm anyway? It seemed deserted. She could be the only person in the entire realm. That would lead to a rather lonely remainder of her life, which wouldn't be all that long if she didn't find some food. Jessica shrugged and kept walking. Hopefully she would come across someone or something soon.

Just when Jessica thought she could take no more, a strange sound rippled through the air. She couldn't place the noise. It wasn't something she had ever heard before and it didn't sound mechanical. But something was making it and that something was getting closer.

She quickly looked around for something to hide behind. There wasn't much, so she dashed behind a small shrub and squatted down. Louder and louder the strange noise became until Jessica thought that whatever it was should be right above her. She looked into the sky and fell to her butt in shock at what she saw there.

Never in her wildest dreams could she have pictured the majestic beast that hovered above her. How had she missed its approach? The thing was huge. Massive in size and the most beautiful green color she had ever seen, the dragon stretched its wings wide and flapped them twice, before landing and folding them against its body.

Jessica peeked at the dragon over the top of the shrub. It was like something out of a storybook. It towered over her in size and its green scales shimmered in the light. It had two long brown horns on either side of its massive head and matching horns on the end of its tail. Two large black eyes stared back at her and she got the feeling that it was an intelligent animal. When it opened its mouth and made a chuffing sound, Jessica covered her ears and shrunk back behind the shrub.

Gosh, she hoped it wasn't a fire-breathing dragon or she was about to be barbecued. When nothing happened, Jessica mustered up the courage to take another look. The dragon lowered its great form toward the ground and then ducked its head until that, too, touched the ground. It reminded Jessica of a puppy that had lain down before pouncing on a toy.

Jessica looked over at the dragon and noticed that it had something on its back. It looked like a person, slumped over in a saddle at the base of its neck. The dragon must be fairly tame, then.

When the person didn't move, Jessica decided to take a closer look. As she slowly approached the dragon, she kept her head down and her hands at her side, taking one step at a time so she didn't spook it and end up getting eaten. Once she was close enough to see the person properly, she saw that it was a woman. She was unconscious, but still alive. Jessica could just make out the shallow breaths she was taking.

How the hell was she supposed to get her down?

"Hello, can you hear me?" She called up to the woman, but got no response. How did she even get herself up there? There was no ladder or anything that she could see. Jessica slowly moved around to the front of the dragon. Her heart was pounding in her chest and she was starting to sweat. The giant beast scared her and she really didn't want to be its next meal, but she knew she had to help the woman.

"Nice dragon, lovely dragon." She spoke in soft tones, trying not to spook it. "I need to help your friend, but I can't get her down. I need your help."

The dragon stared back at her. Its eyes bespoke intelligence and she knew that it understood what she was telling it. It gave a small chuff, nearly knocking her on her ass with the strength of its breath. Shaking its back, much like a dog shaking off water, the woman slumped from the saddle and fell to the ground.

Geez, that was a bit rough. "Thank you, dragon."

It chuffed again, almost a chuckle this time, as Jessica ran to the woman on the ground. As she checked the unconscious form for injury, the dragon swung around to face her, watching her every movement. The woman was young, maybe early twenties, and had long, straight, brown hair. She was wearing a long purple dress that looked medieval in style. It had long sleeves and would fall to her ankles if she were standing, with a rope belt and ribbon tying up the front. She was covered in dirt from head to toe.

There was no sign of external injury, so Jessica knew that whatever was wrong with the woman was on the inside. She loosed the woman's dress and placed her palms flat against her abdomen. Jessica felt the magic pour through her. She opened her senses and tried to read the signals. Shit. This woman wasn't sick, she was dying.

Jessica could feel the poison running through the woman's veins. She didn't have much time. She closed her eyes and concentrated on pulling all the poison from the woman's body and into hers. She didn't stop until she had every last drop. The woman opened her eyes and looked at her. The most violet eyes she had ever seen stared up at her.

"Hi," Jessica squeaked out.

But then she slumped to her side and was out cold.

* * * *

Baen was starting to get worried. They had checked all of his sister's usual haunts and she hadn't been seen at any of them. Where the fuck was she? He was going to lock her in her room when he caught up with her. Marrying her off sounded better and better.

The horses thundered across the ground, the hooves kicking up dirt as they went. They were approaching the border between Marak and the neighboring Barak. Baen had to decide whether or not to cross in search for his sister. If they crossed the border, King Balfour might perceive it as an act of war and use it as an excuse to attack. However, if his sister were over the border, then Baen would be the one attacking.

They rode over a rise and Baen lifted his fist to halt Carr and the men. In the distance Baen could see Knucker, Elvinia's dragon. He could just make out his sister kneeling next to something in front of the dragon. She hadn't crossed the border yet, but she wasn't far from it. That was one less problem he had to deal with.

Knucker let out a chuff and Elvinia stood up. She started to wave her arms frantically, so Baen nudged his horse forward and his men followed. They raced down the slope toward his sister and Knucker stood to his full height. Baen didn't even wait for his horse to come to a complete stop before he was dismounting and rushing to his sister's side.

The dragon had taken a protective stance over his sister and the huddled form of a woman. His men hovered in the distance, too scared to get to close to the huge dragon. Knucker knew him well and so he had no issue when he walked under the dragon's great body. Carr followed closely behind. The dragon also knew him as a friend.

"Oh, brother, thank goodness you came. You have to help this lady. She saved my life. I can't explain how, but one minute I thought I was going to die and the next, I was fine and she was lying on the ground." Elvinia rushed her words. Baen could barely understand her.

"What is wrong with her?" Carr asked from his side. Baen bent down and looked the woman over. He had never seen her before, so she wasn't from court. She was beautiful. Her eyes were closed and her long lashes fanned her delicate cheeks. She had wild curly blonde hair that exploded in ringlets from her head. She wasn't tall, from what he could tell. She was small, petite even. She was wearing strange clothes. Men's clothes. Her blue breeches were made of a ruff material and hugged her legs. She had on a thick jacket and a matching pair of gray boots.

"I think she has been poisoned. It was the weirdest thing. I went to the markets in Arodi and meet up with Aileanna. After a while I was hungry, so I purchased a pastry from one of the stalls. Anyway, that made me thirsty and—"

"What has any of this got to do with the woman?" Baen snapped. His sister could be long-winded sometimes.

"I'm getting to that! So I was thirsty, right, and so Aileanna went and purchased us ale. Which we drank and then went our separate ways. I was on my way home on Knucker when I started to feel sick and—"

"I still do not understand what this has to do with the woman?"

"Enough, Baen, let your sister tell her tale," Carr told him.

"The woman will be dead before she makes her point," Baen replied. He was exasperated with his sister and worried for the lovely lady. He didn't know her, but he didn't want her to die either.

"Anyway, I got sicker and sicker. My stomach was cramping and I was sweating. It was horrible. Then I must have passed out because next thing I know, I was fine and this woman was standing over me with her hands on my stomach. It was like she had pulled the sickness from my body and into hers. Then she said hello and slumped over."

"Who is she? And how could she have done something like that?" Carr asked.

"I have never seen her before, but she is sweating something bad and she was moaning before," Elvinia said. Baen didn't have any idea how to help the woman that had saved his sister's life. He stood up from his crouching position and ran his fingers through his hair in frustration.

"We need to get her back to the castle. Hopefully the healer, Elsbeth, will know what to do." Baen leant down and scooped the small woman into his arms. She was light as a feather and curled into him as he walked toward his mount. Where had she come from? How had she helped his sister that way? Why would she put her life in danger to help a stranger? And who the hell had tried to poison his sister?

Baen had more questions than answers, and the more he thought about it the angrier he became. Someone had tried to kill his baby sister, his only sister. That was an act of war, and when he discovered the culprit they wouldn't be in this world for long.

Baen passed the woman over to Carr as he mounted his stallion and then took her back into his arms. He didn't miss the look of longing on his lover's face when he looked down at the gorgeous woman. He knew just what Carr was thinking. He was thinking it himself. She was a beautiful woman and if her previous actions were anything to go by, she was a brave one too.

He didn't want to explore the emotions he was feeling toward her. She was probably going to die. He needed to concentrate on getting her to the healer and discovering who the enemy was. He couldn't think of how perfect she felt in his arms or how she snuggled into him like a contented kitten. Or how much he wanted her to open her eyes, just so he could see what color they were.

He watched as Carr and the rest of his men mounted their horses and his sister walked back and climbed up Knucker's great height to her saddle. He kicked his horse into a gallop and they were racing toward the castle. Knucker flew over their heads. His great wings flapped as he went higher and higher into the sky.

The dragon would watch after his sister, of that he was sure. They had each been given a dragon egg at birth from the mage Diarmad that resided in their castle. He was a grumpy old man who rarely left his rooms. Baen often sought out his company for either advice or just to talk. The man had been his father's closest friend and had many a tale about their adventures together.

Dragons weren't rare in Marak, but it was uncommon for people to have them as pets. Baen and his sister had been raised with their dragons and each had a special bond because of it. His was a black fire dragon named Nughogg. He lived in a cave, a fair distance from the castle, but all Baen had to do was signal on a horn and he would come.

He had gotten too big to live at the castle by the time Baen was eight, but they had always been friends and he could always rely on his dragon. It was more than the average relationship between owner and pet. Dragons were an intelligent species and they needed to be treated as such. They were big and dangerous and so very stubborn, not unlike him really.

It wasn't long before they were riding over the drawbridge and into the lower bailey. Baen rode all the way to the keep's large wooden doors before dismounting. He rushed the woman through the maze of corridors and into one of the guest chambers, barking orders as he went.

He gently placed her down on the coverlet and then went about making her more comfortable. He removed her knee-length boots and the strange stockings she wore under them. Then he tried to figure out how to remove the tight breeches she wore. They didn't have ties like normal breeches, but a button and a wired metal track that came apart as he pulled on the device holding it together.

He peeled the breeches down her slim legs and tried not to look at the skin he uncovered. His cock sprang to life despite his attempt to keep his desire at bay. She had stunning legs. Slim and slightly muscled with smooth pale skin. Shit, he was supposed to be making her comfortable. He felt like a pervert.

Baen moved up her body and removed her thick jacket, leaving her in her blouse and strange underclothes that covered her womanhood. The little scrap of material was the sexiest thing he had ever seen and his mouth watered at the thought of what lay beneath.

He lifted her gently and tucked her under the blankets. She still hadn't awoken. Baen wasn't sure what poison was given to his sister. If this woman had the power to remove that poison, would it affect her the same way?

Carr burst into the chamber with the healer, Elsbeth, hot on his tail. The woman could sure move for her age. Not that he knew how old she was. She had looked the same for as long as he could remember.

"Move aside, young man, and let me see her," Elsbeth said. Her voice crackled like she had something stuck in her throat. It always gave Baen the urge to cough.

"Has she woken yet?" Carr spoke from his side. Elvinia entered the room and moved to stand on his other side.

"Not as yet. Where are those servants with the water and clothes?" Baen felt useless as he watched her lying in the bed. She looked so small under the covers, the big bed swallowing her up.

"There isn't much I can do for her, unless I know what poison was used. There are a few remedies I will try, but it will come down to her in the end. She needs to be strong to fight it." As Elsbeth spoke, she mixed a purple powder with a few drops of a green liquid in a small bowl. Baen had no idea what the stuff was, but he trusted the healer.

"She is strong. She must be to have the magic to pull poison from a body and into another," his sister put in.

"Has she vomited?" the healer asked. She wrapped her arm around the woman's neck and lifted her head before forcing the mushy paste into her mouth. Baen scrunched up his nose at the foul smell that the paste was producing. It must taste even worse, if it smelt that bad.

"No, she hasn't. She passed out almost immediately."

As Elsbeth forced more of the disgusting potion down the woman's throat, she began to cough and sputter. Opening her eyes, the woman looked around as she spat the paste from her mouth. Rolling to her side, she hung her head from the side of bed before heaving her insides all over the floor.

Carr rushed forward with a cloth and helped wipe her mouth. She took the cloth from Carr and pushed him away. It wasn't long before she was back, spewing and retching the contents of her stomach, making an almighty mess. Baen stood back, his sister covering her mouth and trying not to dry retch at the smell. Once she was finished, again she sat up in the bed and cleaned herself once more.

"God, what was that crap? It tasted worse than eating my mother's Tuna Mornay, and that shit is foul." The woman sat in the big bed and looked at their surprised faces.

"She speaks funny," his sister added. That she did. Baen had no clue what she was talking about. Something to do with dung and her mother's cooking. At least she was alive and talking. She sunk back onto the pillows and moaned. It wasn't a delicate moan, but a great pain-filled moan that belied how serious the woman's situation was.

"Can I have some water, please? My mouth feels like something up and died in it." She stared up at them when no one moved. Baen called for a servant and had them bring a pitcher of water. He couldn't stop staring at the stunning woman. Even covered in sweat, her hair sticking to her forehead and covered in her own vomit, she was lovely. Her large blue eyes looked back at them and he felt himself getting hard again.

Now was not the time or place. Well, maybe the place. They were in a bedchamber after all, but he couldn't help himself. She had stolen all rational thought.

"What is it? Why are you all staring at me like I have two heads?"

Chapter Four

Jessica felt like she had been run over by a steamroller. Her head pounded, her stomach was cramping, and she was drained of energy. The poison had taken its toll and the horrible crap, which the old lady had forced down her throat, didn't help. What she wouldn't give for a bath about now. If only she had the energy to get out of bed.

Now they all stood there staring at her. The old lady that had given her the potion sat next to her, looking down her hawk-like nose. The young woman she had saved stood next to two of the biggest men she had ever seen. Jessica was mortified that the two of the hottest men she had ever laid eyes on had just seen her hurl her guts all over the stone floor. She wanted to hide under the covers until they left. Instead, she had used smart-ass comments and sass to hide her embarrassment.

When nobody answered her question, just continuing to stare at her, she took the time to look over at the two hot men. The one that had called for the water was the taller of the two. He was massive in size, standing at least seven feet tall, and Jessica would bet that the top of her head would barely reach his chest. He was packed with muscles. Wearing a sleeveless white tunic, she wouldn't be able to wrap her hands around half of the expanse of his huge exposed arms. His black breeches molded to his powerful legs. She looked at his muscled thighs before her eyes wandered to his cock. He was well endowed, the size growing beneath his breeches as she watched.

Jessica looked up into his face. He was watching her. His long black hair was tied back away from his strong handsome face. He had seen her looking at him and he was amused. It flashed in his gray eyes, crinkling them at the edges. She tried not to blush, but it was useless. She could feel her face getting hot.

She turned her attention away from the giant man and looked at the other one. Boy, did they grow them big around here. This one was only slightly shorter than the other, and though he, too, was packed with muscles, he wasn't as big or as solid. He had shoulder-length brown hair that he had left down and big brown eyes. He had a scar that ran down the length of his face and made him appear dangerous. Jessica thought it was sexy.

He was dressed much the same as the taller man, but instead of a white shirt, his was black. He still had on the same tight breeches and black boots, but he had a large sword hanging from a thick leather belt around his waist. The steel was incased in an ornamental sheath that depicted dragons entwined in battle. It was really lovely and reminded Jessica of the real dragon she had seen. That bought her back to reality and she stopped perving on the two men and decided to get some answers.

"Please, can you tell me where I am? Who are you people?" she asked. When the scarred man raised an eyebrow, she hoped she hadn't insulted anyone.

"My name is Baen Caladh and you are in my home. The lady on the bed next to you is Elsbeth, our healer." Baen pointed to Elsbeth and then to his brown haired friend. "This is Carr and I presume you know my sister Elvinia."

"You are the woman from the field, the one with the dragon. God, I can't believe I just said that. Dragons are a myth where I come from."

"Where do you come from? How did you end up in Marak?"

"Marak?"

Baen and the man named Carr looked at each other before Baen turned back to her. "Marak is the name of our kingdom, little one. How is it that you have never heard of it?"

"That's a long story," she replied before yawning. She was getting drowsy, not unusual after using her gift. She needed to sleep to recover.

"How was it that you were able to save me?" Elvinia asked.

"We need to get you cleaned up and rested," Carr put in. "There will be time for explanations later."

"But I want to know now!" Elvinia stomped her foot and pouted, but the men were having none of it.

"You will have to wait, Elvinia. The woman saved your life. The least we can do is see her well rested and taken care of before we bombard her with questions."

"I'm sure that she has just as many questions as you do, but they will all have to wait. She needs rest and you will not disturb her. Besides, there is the subject of your punishment to discuss." Baen's voice was strong and authoritative as he spoke. It sent shivers straight down Jessica's back, to her pussy. She had never come across men quite like these two, and despite her exhaustion she was turned on and horny.

His sister paled at her brother's words and Jessica wondered what he had in mind. She didn't think he would hurt her. The love they had for each other was obvious, and, even though danger rippled from the men, she knew that they were honorable. She couldn't explain it if she tried. It was just a gut feeling she had and that had never steered her wrong yet.

"Wait!" she called, when they all turned toward the door to leave. "You haven't even asked me my name yet."

Baen walked back toward the bed, avoiding the mess she had made on the floor. "What is your name, little one?"

"Jessica Whittemore. My name is Jessica."

"Jessica," he said. And then he walked from the room.

Elsbeth helped her change from her soiled clothes into a fresh nightgown and then washed the sweat from her face. She was drained and still feeling sick, so Elsbeth left her to sleep and recover.

Jessica lay in bed and thought about the two men. Servants had entered the chamber and were quietly cleaning the mess she had made on the floor. They didn't speak to her, but she didn't speak to them either. She was too busy fantasizing.

She ran her tongue across the roof of her mouth. God that stuff had been gross. She would have been fine without it. She was working the poison out of her body on her own. That stuff had just made her lose her stomach contents. She never did get that water, even though Baen had asked for it.

Baen had such a deep voice. She could feel the power in every word that he spoke. She could tell he was used to getting his way. She wondered why that was. Maybe he was the lord of this castle.

The other man didn't say much. He must be the dark, silent type. Not much to say and deadly when angered. She was being fanciful, but it was hard not to. She had walked through a veil in the realms and into a land of giants. A land filled with big hard men that fell straight out of a medieval romance novel, complete with dragons.

She thought about what it would be like to have the men's hands on her body. They would be rough and callused from hard work. They would engulf her small breasts and her nipples would pebble under their strong dominant touch. Jessica's pussy dampened and she shifted in the bed.

The men would rip her clothes from her body, exposing her to their gaze. She would spread her thighs wide and let them look at her pussy, wet and swollen. One of the men would shoulder his way between her thighs, and after inhaling her sweet scent would lick her from ass to clit. The other man would be paying homage to her hard pointy nipples, sucking them into the cavern of his mouth and gently biting down.

Jessica closed her eyes as her fantasy got serious. She was so turned on, despite the fact that she didn't know either of the men besides the few minutes she had just spent with them. She needed to stop or she was going to have to finish herself off and she really didn't want to get caught masturbating. That would be humiliating.

She snuggled into the blankets and tried to turn her thoughts away from the men, but it was no use. She kept coming back to them, picturing them in her mind and not wearing their clothes either. Jessica fell asleep with the men on her mind and a smile on her lips.

* * * *

Baen followed behind his sister and Carr as they walked to the great room. It was a large hall in the castle, where they usually held important gatherings. The sidewalls were lined with two doors each and it had three inglenooks that heated the room and gave visitors a warm place to sit. Large tapestries hung from the ceiling and a throne sat on a dais along the back wall.

They didn't use the room much, but he had brought his sister here as a reminder of the importance of her position. She was a princess and she needed to start acting like one. She couldn't go running off without her guard, especially now that someone had made an attempt on her life. He followed her over to one of the inglenooks and then turned to her.

"What the hell did you think you were doing? You are a princess, Elvinia. You can't keep running off without your guard. This is the perfect example of why. What would you have done if Jessica was not there to save you? You would be dead, that is where."

"Brother, please. Knuckers doesn't like the guards and he is more than enough to keep me safe," she said, petulantly.

"Evidence would prove otherwise, sister."

"I'm perfectly capable of looking after myself. Father taught me to fight, just like you."

"You really think you would stand a chance against a man of my size?"

"Of course." Baen couldn't believe what he was hearing. His sister wouldn't even be able to lift the sword that he and his men trained with. It was beside the point anyway.

"The point is moot, sister, especially when the danger is coming from someone that hides in the shadows and uses subterfuge to bring you down. Your ability to fight did not stop someone from poisoning you."

"I want to know if Aileanna had anything to do with it," Carr said from where he sat on one of the benches that surrounded the inglenook.

"Good question. Send men to bring her here for questioning. I want to know what she knows."

"I'll send men for her at once," Carr told him, as he stood and left the room.

"Aileanna would not have anything to do with it. She has been my friend since infancy," his sister added. It didn't matter. He would question her anyway. Trusting no one but his closest men had kept him alive on more than one occasion.

"You will not leave the castle until the culprit is found. If you disobey me, I will lock you in your room and you will stay there for however long it takes to catch them." Baen almost smiled at his sister's indrawn breath. She hated to be confined. She was such a free spirit, craving the adventure of the outdoors.

"I'm telling Mother. She won't let you keep me locked up like a criminal."

"Mother knows who is King, and that my word is law. She won't go against me in this."

"I'll never speak to you again. I hate being cooped up." She was starting to sound whinny now and Baen had had enough. When he spoke she listened. It was the way of things. His sister was still so young in many ways and often acted like it. He couldn't forget that, now that she looked like a woman.

"Enough!" he shouted. "You will do as I say."

Elvinia turned on her heel and stormed from the room, her long hair bouncing behind her. She stomped passed Carr as he returned from his errand and took a seat. She would be in a snit for days, but if it meant that she was safe, he would let her have her tantrum.

He turned to Carr, who had been mostly quiet for the majority of the time. He wasn't one to put himself between family business, despite the fact that Baen considered him as part of his family.

"Elvinia will need to be guarded continuously," Baen told his lover and friend. "I would not put it past her to go off on one of her little capers, despite the danger."

"She is headstrong, that is for sure. Reminds me of someone," Carr said sarcastically. Baen walked toward his lover and knelt down on floor at his feet. He ran his hands along Carr's large muscled thighs.

"The difference, my love, is that I had responsibilities of a kingdom. I had to grow up fast. She has nothing to keep her out of trouble and she grows bored easily." He leant forward and placed his lips over Carr's. He molded their mouths together and drank from his lover's lips.

"Didn't stop you from getting into mischief though, did it?" Carr said between kisses.

"No, but I had you to watch my back. I shall have to speak to Mother. She needs a project. Something to occupy her time."

"Maybe you should have her plan a ball. Invite all the available nobles and see if she can find a match. It will keep her out of trouble and possibly find her a husband all at the same time."

"You have a devilish mind, Carr. My sister will hate the idea. She is determined to stay unwed. It is a sound idea. I will speak to Mother as soon as we finish here." Baen leant forward to take Carr's lips with his once more, but Carr's words interrupted his plans.

"I thought we were finished here?"

Baen smiled and reached for the ties on his lover's breeches.

"Oh no, my love. We are just getting started. I have a serious problem that needs your attention." Baen slid the breeches down Carr's thighs until they pooled around his ankles. He ran his hands along Carr's naked thighs, the coarse hair tickling his palms. When he reached the junction of his thighs, he took the long throbbing cock in his fist and squeezed the long length.

Carr had a magnificent cock. Long and thick, with a large bulbous head, it made Baen's mouth water. He ran his fist up the stalk once more and clear liquid leaked from the slit. Baen leant forward and swiped his tongue across the top of Carr's cock, his masculine flavor exploding in his mouth.

Carr groaned above him, so Baen repeated the action, slowly pumping his fist up and back as he went. Carr shivered and threw his head back, closing his eyes as Baen gently tortured his erection.

"Don't tease me, Baen. Please, suck me," Carr panted out. Baen took the length of his lover cock into his mouth and down to the back of his throat. He started to bob his head up and down. Carr moaned and wiggled above him. Baen loved that he could do this to his lover. Loved that he had the power to bring him pleasure.

He took him to the back of his throat again and then moaned around the length, sending vibrations along the shaft. Carr thrust his hips up in response, so Baen did it again.

"Oh God, Baen. I'm so close. I can't hold it much longer. It feels so fucking good."

Baen smiled as best as he could with his mouth filled with his lover's cock. He tightened his grip and sucked harder, hollowing out his cheeks. He wasn't planning on stopping. He wanted Carr to lose control. Wanted his lover's seed flowing over his tongue.

"Fuck, I going to come. Fuck, Baen. Oh God! Yes!"

Carr grabbed onto handfuls of his hair and took control, thrusting his hips up into Baen's waiting mouth. He wasn't gentle, but Baen didn't care. He loved that he had done this to Carr, driving him beyond control with passion. He would take care of him. Carr could just let go and feel.

It wasn't long before Carr was shouting out his name and Baen felt ropes of pearly essence fill his mouth. He swallowed as more of his lover's cum splashed over his tongue. He loved the flavor of his gentle warrior. He was masculine and strong, and he craved the salty taste.

He licked his lover clean, as Carr panted for breath above him. Baen was nowhere near finished. His cock throbbed in his pants, demanding attention, and he had every intention of seeing to his needs.

* * * *

Carr panted for breath as Baen licked up and down his still-hard cock. Baen was a master at giving head and Carr was always left wrung out and deeply satisfied. He loved it when Baen got like this, all-demanding yet playful at the same time.

Baen also wasn't afraid to make love to him anywhere in the castle. The chance that someone could come along at any moment was a thrill to them both. Carr was more than happy to let Baen take the lead and dictate when and where they made love. Sure, Carr initiated some of their love sessions, but Baen always dominated in the end.

When Baen stood, Carr quickly freed Baen's erection from his breeches and tried to engulf the whole length into his mouth and return the favor.

"No, my love. I need to be inside that ass of yours. Remove the rest of your clothes, whilst I get the grease." Carr rushed to comply and then lay on the rug by the fire. Baen returned to his side after getting the grease they had stashed in a box behind the throne. They had jars of the stuff, placed all over the castle. It was becoming a joke between Baen and himself, the amount of different rooms that they kept it in.

"You make a tempting picture, laid out on the fur rug. I wish I could commission a painting of you, all naked and waiting for my touch." Baen dropped the grease on the rug and stood back to watch him. Carr felt himself blush at Baen's words. He was a big, scarred warrior, but Baen made him feel like he was the best-looking man to walk the Earth and Carr loved him for it. It might not be true, but Carr still appreciated the sentiment.

"Hurry, Baen, I need you to make love to me. I want to feel that big cock pound me into the rug," Carr said, as he watched Baen rip off his clothes and then flop onto the rug next to him. He pulled Baen into his arms and took his mouth. Their tongues tangled and Baen nipped his bottom lip to show his dominance.

Baen pushed Carr onto his back. The fur rug felt soft against his skin. Carr's heart pounded in his chest and his cock throbbed despite the fact that he had just come moments before. He ran his callused hands over the smooth skin of Baen's back and down to his tight firm ass. He squeezed the twin globes between his hands and grinded his hips up to mash his pelvis with Baen's.

"Does my big warrior need something?" Baen asked, as he broke the kiss and sat up.

"Please, Baen, no more teasing. Just fuck me, please." Carr was begging and he knew it, but he needed to feel his lover in his ass in the worst way. He wanted the connection, needed the connection that only Baen could give him.

"You need to learn patience, my lover. Luckily for you, I am just as impatient to be inside you as you are to have me there." Baen grabbed his legs and spread them, revealing his puckered hole to his gaze. He opened the grease jar and scooped some onto his long fingers. Baen leant over Carr's body and started to make love to his mouth again, all the while circling his hole with his finger.

The kiss had Carr's heart racing in his chest again and the teasing fingers at his opening were driving him wild. Carr raised his legs in invitation and groaned when Baen took the hint and pushed two long fingers into his waiting hole.

Carr withered and shook as Baen scissored his fingers in and out, stretching Carr and preparing him for his cock. Carr's cock was hard and throbbing and demanding attention where it lay against his belly between them. He knew that if Baen didn't take him soon, he would be disgracing himself all over his stomach.

It was always like this between them. One touch and he was wild for Baen, desperate for his lover's touch and kiss. Despite the length of time they had been together, the passion they had for each other never waned, only grew stronger in its intensity.

Carr knew Baen was just as needy as him when he lined his cock up with Carr's opening. He slowly moved forward until his big head popped through the tight ring of muscle. Baen then pushed his hips forward until he was all the way inside.

Carr groaned when Baen stilled his movements once more. He wanted to be fucked and fucked hard, but Baen was still teasing him and it was making him crazy.

"Baen, please. You need to move, now," Carr pleaded.

"Soon, my lover. When I'm ready. When I make sure you're ready."

"I'm ready. I'm ready, please. Fuck me."

Baen chuckled down at him, but complied and started to snap his hips back and forth, driving his cock into Carr before retreating again. Yes, he thought, this was what he wanted. Carr groaned and grabbed onto Baen's ass checks as he slammed into him. He threw his head back and felt Baen suck on the exposed flesh of his neck. He was going to have a mark.

"You feel so good, Carr. Come with me." Baen's voice was gruff with passion. A passion that Carr was feeling every bit as much as Baen.

"Oh yes, Baen. I'm almost there," Carr cried. Baen's hips continued to piston into him, driving him closer and closer to orgasm.

Carr reached between their bodies to take his cock in his palm. Baen lifted slightly to give him room, as he started to move his fist up and down.

"Fuck, that's hot," Baen told him. "I'm coming, my love."

Carr felt Baen's cock swell to an even greater size before erupting into his passage. Baen roared out his completion and his whole body shook from the force. The sight was all it took to set Carr off, and with a roar of his own his seed shot from his cock onto his stomach and chest.

Chapter Five

Carr lay curled in his lover's arms. After their bout of rough lovemaking they had collapsed onto the fur rug and Baen had fallen asleep. He looked at his lover's face relaxed in sleep. His long lashes lay fanned on his checks and the hard lines around his eyes had softened. He knew Baen carried a heavy burden as king and didn't envy him his position. All he could do was offer his support and advice whenever Baen needed it.

He would offer his ass whenever Baen needed it, too. He was a demanding lover, but Carr didn't mind. He loved the passion that Baen displayed when they were intimate. He would do anything for this incredible man.

Baen liked to be the one on top, the one in control when they made love, and Carr was more than happy to let him lead. Oh, he liked to be in control every now and then, but Baen wasn't that into it, so Carr only asked on special occasions. That made it all the more special. When he did finally get his cock into his lovers waiting hole, he savored the experience, knowing it might be awhile before Baen let him do it again.

Carr smiled and brushed the hair back from Baen's forehead. He was starting to get cold despite the heat coming off his lover and the roaring fire at his back. This room was always cold. The whole castle was. It never got hot in Marak. The weather was always chilly and it snowed in the winter months.

He wondered if the woman was all right. She might be cold too, and after the ordeal she had been through she needed to be pampered. She had saved the princess's life. That meant that they were indebted to her. Carr would make sure she got everything her little heart desired. It was the least they could do, as far as he was concerned.

She was such a small thing. A strong wind would knock her over. She wouldn't survive the harsh winters if they didn't get some meat on her bones. He would make it his responsibility to make sure she was looked after and that no harm came to her. If that meant that she needed to be coddled and pampered, then that's what he would do.

It didn't help that he was attracted to the woman. She was gorgeous with all that wild curly hair and those big blue eyes. He knew that Baen had felt an attraction too. His lover had looked stunned when he had first looked at her. He had acted very possessive when they were bringing her back to the castle. Maybe they had found their third after all.

No, Carr was getting ahead of himself. She had come to them in strange circumstances and they didn't even know who she was or where she was from. She could already belong to someone. That would devastate him and he hadn't even spoken a word to her yet.

Baen opened his eyes and smiled up at Carr. Baen had the most stunning gray eyes. Carr could stare into them all day. Carr leant down and placed a small kiss on his lips.

"What has you so deep in thought, my lover?" Baen asked. He didn't wait for his reply, standing up and pulling on his clothes. Carr stood too and also proceeded to get dressed.

"I was thinking of our little visitor and what the future may hold." Carr pulled on his boots and looked over at Baen. He was fully dressed and leaning against the mantel.

"She has done us a great service in rescuing my sister." Baen looked thoughtful. "We need to question her, before we do anything else. Find out where she came from and how she was able to do what she did."

"I was thinking the same thing myself. I was also thinking what a beautiful woman she is." Carr watched Baen carefully to see the reaction to his words. When Baen smiled in response, Carr knew he was onto something.

"She could have someone waiting for her. She might not even be attracted to us. I don't want you to get disappointed," Baen told him.

"I saw how she looked at us. She was attracted. She undressed you with her eyes, despite the fact that she was exhausted and had just gone through an ordeal." Carr moved to stand in front of his lover and took his hands in his. "What are we going to do about her then?"

"Marry her, I suppose."

"That might be complicated," Carr said at Baen's flippant reply.

"Yes, but I've never let that stand in my way before," Baen said smugly. Carr pulled Baen into his embrace and hugged him tight.

"I love your optimism. But let's wait until we at least talk to her before we announce our engagement." Baen let out a mighty laugh.

"I love you, Carr. You mean the world to me." Baen placed another long kiss to Carr's lips. He pulled back and released him from his embrace. If they didn't stop they would both be naked again.

"I love you, too." Carr took Baen's hand as they walked toward the door. Exiting the great hall, they made their way toward the guest chamber and hopefully their future.

"Let the wooing begin."

* * * *

Jessica woke as she heard the door to her chamber quietly open. The young woman she had rescued stuck her head in through the doorway.

"Oh good, you're awake!" she said, and then walked further into the room, shutting the door behind her.

Jessica tried to sit up, but was still too drained to make more than a feeble effort. She gave up and lay there looking up at the woman. She had walked over and taken a seat next to the large bed.

She was a lovely woman. Her long black hair flowed freely down her back and she had striking violet eyes. She was wearing another long medieval-style dress. This one was a deep red and had emerald-green panels running down the length of the dress on both sides. It was held together at the front by ties that ran from her waist to chest. This time, instead of a rope belt at her waist, she wore a gold-link chain, which had a large ruby where the belt joined together.

Jessica could see the resemblance between this young woman and the giant man from before. They both had the same coloring and facial features, but this woman was pale and smooth, where as the man was tanned and hard.

"I know my brother said to leave you alone, but I just had to meet you. I am desperate to know how you were able to draw the poison from my body to yours. Are you a witch?" The woman had a soft and lyrical voice. She spoke quickly, her words almost tripping over each other, and she bounced in her seat as she talked.

"No, I'm not a witch. I don't know how I can do it, it is just something I have always been able to do," she replied. "I have questions of my own."

"Ask me anything you like."

"Your name is Elvinia, yes? And we are in a realm called Marak?" Elvinia was nodding her head yes as she spoke, but pulled a face when she said the word "realm."

"Marak is our kingdom, it's not a realm. My brother Baen is the king. How is it that you have never heard of it? Are you from a land on the other side of the Great Sea?"

"No, I'm from a place called England. It is hard to explain. I come from a realm called Earth…"

"But this is Earth. I've never heard of England. It must be over the great sea."

"It's not over the great sea. You see, I came through a gateway, a veil in between my Earth and yours. Now I'm stuck and can't get back through."

"A gateway? I've never heard of such a thing. You must possess great magic to be able to do that. I bet the mage will know. He knows everything."

"That's just it. I'm not that magical. I mean, I can feel when magic is near and I have the ability to pull sickness from people's bodies into mine and then expel it back out, but that's it. I knew nothing of other realms until I stepped into yours."

"Does it make you sick? Because I thought you were going to die for sure."

"I get sick, yes, and it takes an awful lot of energy to use my ability. But no, I don't think it will kill me. It hasn't yet."

Elvinia looked thoughtful as she sat there and looked back at Jessica. She was just as confused as she was and knew she wasn't going to get the answers she sought. She would have to go and see this mage. Maybe he could tell her more.

"Why did someone try and kill you?"

"My brother Baen is King. He has many enemies and they are trying to get his throne. I don't know who would want me dead. It wouldn't gain them anything. It would just hurt my family, if I died."

"Do you have any enemies?" Jessica didn't know why anyone would want to kill this sweet young woman. She seemed harmless and what would be the point? Wouldn't it be more beneficial to take her hostage if they wanted to get to the brother?

"No, I haven't done anything to gain enemies. I suppose my brother's enemies are mine as well, but I still don't know who would want to kill me. To tell you the truth, I'm scared. No one has tried to harm me before, and the thought that someone wants me dead gives me the chills." Jessica thought that Elvinia looked like she was about to cry and who could blame her? If she hadn't been there, she could very well be dead. She decided to change the subject.

"Tell me about Marak," she said. She couldn't do anything until she gained back her strength and so she decided that she would learn as much as she could about this new place.

"Well, there isn't much to say. We are a small kingdom that sits between Barak and Zarak. They are both our enemies. And the great sea is on the south border. To the north there is a great cliff that is the border to Tarak. They aren't our enemies. They are rarely seen because the cliff is so hard to pass."

It sounded bad to Jessica to have so many enemies. If Zarak and Barak ever joined forces, Marak would be stuck in the middle.

"Why are Barak and Zarak you're enemies?"

"Not sure, really," Elvinia replied. "They have been our enemies long before I was born. Something to do with my grandfather. His wife was from Zarak and that meant an alliance. But it all feel apart when the queen accused my grandfather of having a dalliance with a princess from Barak."

"Sounds very 'Days of Our Lives'."

"What? I don't understand."

"Never mind. What about the dragons? Does everybody have dragons?" She was fascinated about the dragons. There must have been a time when the realms were more accessible. The myth about dragons had to come from somewhere. Maybe they came from here and went through the veil and back. Or maybe when they were dying off they fled here. Who knew?

"Dragons are all over Marak. It's just that not all are tame. My brother and I both have pet dragons because we were raised with them. Otherwise they are hard to tame and can be aggressive."

Wow, real-life dragons.

"You will have to take me to meet your dragon again. He was magnificent."

"Yes and doesn't Knuckers know it."

Just as Jessica opened her mouth to ask another question, the door to the chamber opened once more and the two men from before walked in. Jessica was once again struck at how big the men were. They were good looking men and made her heart race and her pussy dampen, just looking at them.

"What do you do here, sister? You were told to leave her to rest," Baen's voice boomed as he scolded his sister.

"I might ask the same of you, brother," Elvinia responded. She stood up from the chair and approached her brother, with her hands on her hips. "You can't seem to keep your distance either."

"Leave us, please. I'll deal with your conduct later." Baen towered over the smaller Elvinia, but she wasn't intimated.

"I'll leave, but only because I don't want to be in the same room as you any longer than necessary." With that she flounced from the room. The man called Carr was trying to hold back a grin. Baen just looked exasperated.

Jessica pulled the covers up to her chin when both of the large men turned to look at her. She was so overwhelmed by their sheer immensity. She knew they wouldn't hurt her, but they were just so goddamn big.

"How are you feeling, little one?" Baen asked as he approached the bed. He sat down in the seat that his sister had just vacated and Carr moved to stand behind him.

"Drained of energy, but the nausea is gone." She really didn't know what to say to them. She didn't want to make a fool of herself by saying something stupid.

"I'm glad you are feeling much better. I wanted to thank you for saving my sister's life. It was a brave thing you did, even if I'm not sure exactly what you did."

"I kind of come from a different realm." Jessica explained her ability to them and then went on to tell them where she came from. She was surprised when they didn't look at her like she had lost her marbles. *I come from a different realm* is not something that people usually start a conversation with.

"Diarmad, the mage, has told tales of people that have fallen through gateways from other realms, but I always thought it a myth," Carr offered. "Remember the one about the man who fell through the realm and was taken by the king, your grandfather, who was going to have him executed as a spy? Only he vanished, before they could cut his head off. Disappeared right from the gallows."

"Yes, I do remember. He said he was from a place called America or some such nonsense. But Grandfather's spies said he had arrived by boat from across the great seas."

Great, she had landed in a realm that still executed people. She shouldn't be surprised, since they were so archaic. They had no technology, dressed like they came straight from a renaissance fair, and still carried swords.

"Do you still execute people?"

"No, my father had that abolished when he was king," Baen replied.

Good, she hated the thought that these two men had lynched or beheaded people in such a barbaric way.

"America is a country from my Earth. They were probably telling the truth." Jessica was starting to get tired again. Expelling the poison from her body had taken its toll. It must have been a strong poison. Whoever had given it to the princess must have wanted her dead, not just sick.

"I need to get home. People will be worried about me." Jessica knew that when she was discovered missing from the bus tour a search would be called. She would be declared a missing person and her friend Elise would be frantic. Who would look after her cat?

"Are you spoken for? Is there a man waiting for you?" Carr asked her. He was wearing a dark scowl and didn't look pleased with the prospect. Baen didn't either for that matter.

"No, there is no man waiting for me. No family either. Just my friend Elise, who works at my store." Jessica had always led a rather lonely life. She had her store and her cat and that was it. She didn't mind. She liked it that way. It was less complicated. Both her parents had passed away, her father in a workplace accident when she was a young girl and her mother from a broken heart, when she was just out of school. The doctors had said it was heart failure, but since the death of her dad, her mum's health had deteriorated. No matter how much she had tried to help her, it was no use.

"Once you are feeling up to it, we will take you to see Diarmad. He will be able to tell you more. He is a very powerful mage and knows a lot about magic. He will be interested to meet you and discuss your abilities," Baen told her. She was interested in meeting the mage as well. She had many questions to ask him, about magic and her ability and if he had ever met anyone like her.

Jessica had asked around the magical community in her realm and had scoured the Internet for information, but if there were people with abilities similar to hers, they weren't talking about it. From what she had discovered, most people back home had no real magical abilities at all and just dallied with spells and such. She would be naive to believe that to be true though. She didn't broadcast her ability and she had seen too much that people couldn't explain to think that she was the only person with any real magical capability.

"Jessica, we will do everything we can to help you, but we want you to be prepared in the event that you are unable to find a way home." Baen leant forward in his seat and took her hand in his. It looked so small and delicate in his large scarred one. She felt a zing shoot through her body at his gentle touch.

"I understand. I think I have already resigned myself to the fact that I might be stuck here. It was a risk I took when I went through the veil. I'm not sure what I'll do, if I can't get home." Jessica was confused. Confused about her future and confused about the feelings she was having for these two men. Two men she barely knew.

"No matter what happens, little one, Carr and I will always look after you. You saved my sister's life, and that is a debt I cannot repay." Baen lifted her hand to his lips and placed a small kiss on her fingers. His lips were soft as he placed them against her skin. She felt it all the way down to her pussy. It throbbed for attention. She wanted those soft lips on her delicate folds.

Jessica shook off the sensual thought and looked at Baen. He was smiling down at her like he knew exactly what she was thinking. She felt herself go red and looked away, straight into the eyes of Carr. He stood behind Baen's chair, with his hands resting on Baen's shoulders. God, they were both so good looking and if she had the strength she would invite them both into her bed.

Well, that wasn't true. She would want to, but she would never have the courage to be so bold with men as tempting as these two.

"Thank you, that means a lot to me. I was given this magic to help people. Your sister wasn't at fault. I don't know why she was poisoned or by who, but I think she was used to hurt you. Maybe she was an easier target, I don't know." Jessica was embarrassed by her outburst. She looked away from the men and hoped they didn't take offence to a woman who had an opinion.

"You are very insightful, little one," Baen told her. She let out a gush of breath in relief. "Whomever it was, is a coward. I hate to admit that ruling a kingdom brings with it many enemies. Some more despicable than others, it would seem."

"If whoever did this finds out you helped Elvinia, your life could well be in danger too," Carr added. "You will need to be protected, every bit as much as she does."

Jessica felt chills go up her spine at his words. She didn't want to get involved in a war that had nothing to do with her. It was like on Star Trek, the Prime Directive and all that. It dictates that there can be no interference with the internal development of other planets. Jessica felt it applied here—don't get involved with the internal struggle that doesn't involve your realm. Yet by rescuing Elvinia, she already had.

"There is only one way that I can protect you and make sure that no one, not even the citizens of Marak, can cause you harm. You will be my wife." Baen stood after his massive declaration and looked down at Jessica. She stared back at him with her mouth flapping open and closed, but no words came out.

"I will make the preparations at once, Your Majesty," Carr said, then rushed from the room.

Did he really just say that they were getting married? What happened to helping her get home? And how on Earth, or Marak in this case, did getting married protect her?

"Hang on, wait a minute. I don't understand. How is getting married going to keep me safe?" she asked. She was confused and she felt helpless being so drained of energy. She wanted to argue, but couldn't even sit up in bed.

"There are people out there, even amongst my nobles, that would do anything to advance their situation. If they discover that you are from another realm they might try and use that to their advantage. As my wife you will be queen and no one will be able to touch you. They would have to get through Carr and myself first."

"Queen!"

Well shit.

Jessica knew that by marrying the king she would be a queen, but she hadn't really thought of it like that until he had said it. What did she know about being a Queen? She knew very little about Marak and its people.

Marrying Baen was a crazy idea. She had to find a way home. She needed to rest and gain her strength back. Then she had to get out of here. She wasn't going to wander around Marak alone, not with all the enemies that were about, but she did need to actively search for a gateway home.

Queen. That was the craziest thing anyone had ever said to her and she worked in a magic shop. It was filled with crazy people and their weird stories. The things people chose to tell her were amazing. Some were so silly that she had to leave the room so she didn't insult them by laughing in their faces. Her customers took their magic very seriously, even if she thought they were ridiculous. She always listened though. They were her bread and butter and so she tried to treat them all with respect.

Jessica lay there long after Baen and Carr had left. She was still tired, but her brain wouldn't shut down. They had dropped their bombshell and then left and now all she could think about were Baen and Carr.

If she married Baen, then she would always be watching Carr and wanting him too. She was attracted to both the men and didn't want to pick one over the other. Jessica knew that Baen hadn't really chosen her. He was just marrying her for safety or some such nonsense, but that didn't mean she could just turn off her attraction to Carr.

What was she talking about? She couldn't marry, but the thought wouldn't leave her alone. And then one thing led to another and she was thinking about them naked again. How she would love to see their muscles ripple as they climbed onto the bed toward her, their long cocks hard and pointing at her, ready to make wild love to her.

She would take Baen's long black hair and run it between her fingers, just to see if it was as soft as it looked. It would fall over her like a veil when he leant down to kiss her. Oh, she would gasp when Carr parted her thighs and looked at her most feminine part. God, she had lost the plot and it was all because of two huge scarred men and an uncontrollable attraction to them, which would bring her nothing but heartache.

No, she needed to focus and set her mind to finding a way home, back to her shop and her cat. It might be a mundane and somewhat boring life, but it was hers.

Chapter Six

Jessica was still in shock four days later. Baen had declared that they would marry and she hadn't seen him or Carr since. She had spent most of the time sleeping, but they still should have come at least once. Elvinia had visited often and kept her informed of her brother's arrangements.

She was feeling stronger now and able to sit up in bed and take small walks around the room. She still tired easily and slept a lot, but was well on the way to recovery. She was getting cabin fever though. She hated to be so indisposed and was going to use what little strength she had to get out of this room and talk to the king.

She had to change his mind. Marrying her was impossible. She tried to understand his reasoning, but she didn't. She needed to find a way home. How would he explain that to his people, when the queen just up and left one day?

Queen, she still couldn't wrap her mind around that. He wanted to make her the queen of a kingdom she knew nothing about, all because she had saved his sister life and he felt he owed her a debt. Well, he would just have to find another way to repay it and another way to protect her. She wasn't going to tie herself to someone she barely knew. She wouldn't marry for anything less than love. No matter how hot she thought him or how badly she wanted to get him between the sheets.

She needed to tell him before things got out of hand. He had already called together the nobles to make his intention of marriage known. Elvinia had said that she had never seen her brother so determined on a course of action. She had a battle ahead of her if she was going to get him to back down.

Jessica slowly got out of bed and removed her nightgown. She slipped the chemise over her head and then put on the outer gown. The gown fell all the way to the floor and was a deep ruby red with a white front panel. She tied up the red ties on the front and slipped the rope belt around her waist and adjusted it to sit on her hip. The sleeves on the gown were large, the ends dangling almost to the floor.

She would have to get used to wearing such an unusual dress. She felt like a little girl in a fairytale. The material was velvet and so smooth under her hands. It must have cost a fortune, but Elvinia had given it to her with no qualms. She slipped on the matching red slippers and she was exhausted.

Jessica had second thoughts about leaving the room, and almost got back into bed. She could always wait one more day or two. No, she had to put an end to this now before she ended up walking down the aisle. She made her way to the large wooden door and slowly turned the iron handle.

It creaked open and she stuck her head out. She felt like a thief, sneaking around like she was. She gave herself a mental slap on the cheek and exited the room. Jessica had no idea where she was going as she walked down the long corridor. There was no one around to ask, so she just kept walking.

Jessica came to a long winding staircase and looked down. Grabbing on to the wall for support, she slowly started her descent. When she got to the bottom, she saw another long corridor. God, this was going to take forever. She had to take three breaks to rest on the staircase alone. The damned castle was huge. She kept going, poking her head in and out of rooms looking for someone, anyone who could tell her where to go to find the King.

She had just about made it to the end of the corridor when she stopped in front of two wide doors. She could hear voices on the other side, but was unable to tell what they were saying. Jessica felt scared to walk through the door and ask for help, but she didn't know if she could go on much further. She either had to get someone to take her to the king or get them to take her back to her room. Either way she needed help.

Mustering all her courage, she turned the knob and walked into the room. Jessica stopped in her tracks the moment she entered. It was some sort of long meeting room. It had a large table in the center and a fireplace at the end. Men, now all looking at her, took up all the chairs. Baen stood at the head of the table, with Carr seated to his right.

"What are you doing out of bed, little one?" Baen's voice boomed through the room and he didn't sound happy. He turned back to address the men. "We will discuss this further later."

Carr stood and followed Baen as he approached her. He didn't slow as he scooped her up in his arms and walked from the room.

"You should be resting. You aren't strong enough yet. You were swaying on your feet."

"What made you leave your chamber, baby?" Carr asked. "If you needed something, you should have had one of the servants fetch us."

"I can't stay in bed anymore. I'm going crazy. I need to speak to you." She wrapped her arms around Baen's neck and held on. She was so far off the ground, he was so damned tall. Jessica hadn't been carried around like this since she was a little girl. She wasn't sure whether she liked it or not. She wasn't one to rely on others when she was capable of doing things herself, but it felt really good to be in his arms.

"You still should have sent for us. As your intended husband, it is my responsibility to see to your well-being and happiness." Jessica looked up at Baen as he spoke. She was lost in the depth of his amazing gray eyes. She knew she was supposed to be protesting his claim on her, but when he looked at her with those startling eyes, she lost all train of thought.

Jessica expected Baen to take her back to her chamber, but when he entered another room, she was surprised. It was another chamber and Jessica suspected it was his. Twice the size of the room she had been given, it had the biggest bed she had even seen. The four-poster bed took up only a small amount of space in the large room, but would easily fit five people lying side by side comfortably. It was adorned with a deep emerald-green spread with gold trimming.

The rest of the room was furnished just as opulently. Two large wooden wardrobes with elegant carvings lined the wall next to the bed. A fireplace on the opposite wall to the bed had a chaise lounge in front. There was a large desk in the corner and a huge fur rug in the middle of the room. Once again tapestries depicting war scenes hung from the wall, and the widows were covered with long flowing curtains that matched the bedspread.

He walked further into the room and placed her down on the chaise by the fire. She was instantly warmed from the heat. When he stood back, Jessica tried to sit up, but one shake of his head had her freezing.

"We will accommodate you, Jessica, and let you have your talk. But you will do it lying down and resting." Baen's deep voice sent shivers down her spine and made her pussy weep and throb for attention. How did he do that? He was ordering her around and she was getting turned on.

"What was it you wanted to say, baby?" Carr asked. He dragged over a chair and motioned for Baen to sit down before getting one for himself. Even though they were sitting down, they still towered over her. She scooted up a little on the lounge, but it was no use. She still felt small and had to look up at them.

"It's about this whole marriage thing. I still don't think it's the best course of action. It would be silly for you to marry me and then for me to go home, and you're left alone again. How would you explain it to people?"

"You let me and Carr worry about that, little one. You just have to get well enough to walk down the aisle. We will take care of everything else. Besides, it is a possibility that you will be unable to go home."

"That's another thing. When are you going to take me to see Diarmad?"

"We will take you to see him this afternoon. As long as you rest." Baen leant forward and tucked a loose strand of hair behind her ear. Jessica felt the touch all through her body and she lost her train of thought again. The men sure did know how to distract her. She opened her mouth to reprimand him, but he was too quick. Wrapping a hand around the back of her neck, he lifted her slightly and placed his lips over hers.

His lips were soft, but his kiss firm. When she gasped in surprise, he took advantage to thrust his tongue into her mouth. The longer he kissed her the more she relaxed and soon she was kissing him back and tangling her tongue with his. She moaned into his mouth and wrapped her arms around his neck to pull him closer.

Jessica felt the kiss all the way to her toes. Her nipples hardened and her pussy gushed once more. Her body was priming itself for lovemaking and Jessica was more than willing to go along for the ride.

Baen placed his free hand on her waist, before moving it slowly up her body to cup her breast. His hand was big and engulfed her breast in his entire palm. When he pinched her nipple, she almost shot off the chaise. She moaned loudly again and sucked hard on his tongue.

When Baen finally lifted his head, she sunk back into the soft cushions of the chaise lounge. Baen's eyes were dazed and passion-filled as he looked down at her and she knew hers would be the same. Boy, did the man know how to kiss.

"That was something else, my love. Out of the way and let me have a turn." Carr's voice broke them both out of their kiss-induced spell. Jessica looked up at Carr as he took Baen's spot in front of her. Did he really mean to kiss her too?

The answer was obvious as Carr scooped Jessica up in his arms and slammed his mouth down on hers. His kiss was every bit as demanding as Baen's. But where Baen stroked and suckled, Carr dueled and nipped. He paid a lot of attention to her bottom lip, sucking it into his mouth and biting it.

Jessica felt his kiss every bit as much as Baen's and, though different, it was just as seductive and powerful. Carr pulled her closer in his arms and Jessica clung back, moaning and withering. They needed to stop this now or Jessica was going to rip off all their clothes and have her way with them.

Carr broke the kiss and gently let Jessica fall back onto the chaise. He smiled down at her and her heart lurched. She looked away, unsure of how they both could affect her so much. She had lost all reasonable thought when they had kissed her. It was frightening and exciting at the same time.

"I…err…I…" Jessica didn't know what to say. Both men had just kissed her senseless and she had loved every minute of it. Wait a minute. They had *both* just kissed her. Why would Carr be kissing her when she was supposed to be engaged to Baen?

"You just kissed me! And you just let him. Oh God. I'm so confused." Jessica sat up on the chaise lounge and glared at the men.

"Calm down, baby, and I'll explain." Carr sat forward and took both of her hands in his larger ones. "Baen and I have been together for quite a few years now and I love him very much."

"Oh, so this will be a marriage of convenience? That still doesn't explain why you kissed me."

Baen smirked at her from where he sat next to Carr, but didn't say anything.

"Stop interrupting, woman. We have been waiting for the right lady to come along. A woman who will complete us. Baby, Baen and I think that you are that lady."

"I'm sorry. Did I just hear you right? You both want to be with me?" Jessica was shocked. Not about both of them wanting to share a woman, but that they wanted to share her.

"Yes, little one. You will be married to both of us and we will be married to each other," Baen added. "Marrying Carr is something I should have done many years ago."

"You don't need to marry me to marry Carr though, do you? I still don't see—"

"Baby, we aren't going to marry you as some sort of intrigue. We want to marry you because we are attracted to you. We admire your bravery and your spirit. Both Baen and I think with you at our side we could lead a very complete and happy life."

Jessica felt tears well in her eyes. Nobody had ever said anything so sweet to her before. They were chipping away at her defenses and she so badly wanted to say yes, but she needed to go home. She had a life back in Notting Hill, albeit not a very full one, but it was hers and she needed to get back to it.

"I'm not sure I can give you what you need. I'm not as wonderful as you make me out to be." Jessica felt her heart break with every word she spoke. She didn't want to reject these men, the first men to take notice of her attributes and not think she was strange. "But I need to figure a way to get home."

"Don't say no, little one. Give us a chance whilst we try and find you a way home, and if when the time comes and you still want to go home, we will let you." Baen said.

"We will still have to marry to keep you safe, that hasn't changed. But let us woo you and then decide." Jessica nodded at the men. She would let them have their way for now but she would harden her heart to their attentions and not fall in love with them, not if she could help it.

Carr kissed her lips and then stood. Baen followed him toward the door. When they reached it, Baen turned back to face her.

"Try and rest, little one. We will handle the rest. Later we will take you to see Diarmad." With that they were gone. Jessica couldn't help but feel that she had disappointed them somehow. She had been honest from the start that she had to go home. It was their crazy idea that she give up everything that she had ever known and stay with them. Despite her determination to get back to her shop and her realm, Jessica couldn't help but wonder what life would be like if she stayed.

The men were both so strong and dominant. Her life wouldn't be her own. She would be constantly guarded, and, because she would be queen, constantly in danger. The kingdom had enemies and was still at war. What happened if the men were killed in battle? She would be left in realm she knew nothing about, alone. No, she may think these men were hot as all get out and she may even be falling for them, but staying here wasn't an option. It was just too different. She had to find a way home, no matter how badly she wanted to stay.

* * * *

Carr walked into the mage's chambers and called out to Diarmad. Baen and Jessica followed closely behind him. Carr was still reeling over the kiss they had shared. He had never been that affected by a kiss before. When he was with Baen, there was passion and he was turned on, but nothing as mind-blowing as what he had experienced with Jessica. He had told Baen about it and he had said he had the same explosive feelings. They decided it was nothing to do with what they felt for each other and that it was because it was new.

Carr hoped that they were right. He would hate if his longing for the little curly-haired woman caused trouble for him and Baen. It was unlikely. Their love was strong and they were open with all their feelings.

Diarmad answered Carr the second time he called out, and emerged from the small sleeping area. His chambers were divided up into two separate sections. The smaller one he used as sleeping quarters. It was only big enough to hold a small cot and thin wardrobe. The larger space was used to hold all Diarmad's potions and the ingredients that he needed. There was a large fireplace on the wall opposite the door. The rest of the room was lined with shelves and an old rickety table sat in the middle.

Baen had offered to move Diarmad to a larger room on numerous occasions, but he had wanted to stay where he was. He said that it would upset his magic and it had taken him years to get the vibe just right.

"What can I do you for, my friends?" Diarmad asked, then crossed over to sit by the fire. Age was catching up to the old man. He was thin and frail, and used a long stick to walk around. His hair had long gone gray and his face was droopy and weathered.

"We want you to meet someone, old man." Carr dragged Jessica forward to stand next to him. "This is Jessica, Baen's and my intended."

Diarmad stared up at her and didn't say anything. His eyes glazed over and he appeared in a trance. Carr had never seen anything like it. It was spooky and unnerving to watch. Carr was starting to get worried when he finally spoke.

"The magic is strong in you, young lady. You will be a great asset to our realm. You will do many great things. Your kin will be powerful and rule the kingdom for years to come." Diarmad's eyes returned to normal as he shook off the trance. He looked up at them and smiled. "Cup of tea? You will, you will."

He turned toward the fire and placed an old black kettle on the flames.

"Now, what can I do for you, young folk?" Diarmad didn't appear to remember anything he had just said.

"What did you mean, just now? About my kin being powerful? It was the trippiest thing I have ever seen." Jessica stood by his side, so he grabbed her hand in his own, entwining their fingers. He was thrilled when she didn't pull away. She was right though, even if she had a funny way of putting it. What Diarmad had just done was weird.

"What? I didn't say anything. Just asked if you wanted tea. You're a strange girl," he said, then turned to Baen. "Where did you find this one, Baen? She is positively disturbed." Carr held back a smile. Diarmad was always one to speak his mind.

"It wasn't just her, my old friend. We heard it too. You just went into a trance and spoke of the future. Told Jessica her powers were strong."

"Come here, girl. Let me see you. I'll be the judge of whether or not your magic is strong." Carr was starting to think this was the strangest audience he had ever had with the mage. He let go of her hand and gently shoved her toward Diarmad. She walked slowly toward him, her steps hesitant. When she finally made it over to the old man, he took her hand in his and she squatted down in front of him.

"Yes, yes, yes. I see..." He scrunched his face up in concentration. "The water's ready." He let go of her hand and removed the kettle from the heat. Jessica stood up and moved back to their side.

"What do you see, old man? Spit it out, already," Baen said. Carr could tell that Baen was getting frustrated. He never snapped at the mage. He was his father's oldest friend and deserved respect. But he certainly was acting odd today.

"Oh, well. This young lady has magic in her veins, that's for sure. How do you take your tea?" They were getting nowhere. Maybe they should come back another day.

"Diarmad, have you ever heard of gateways to other realms? Have you ever heard of England?" Jessica asked. She was polite and thanked the mage when he handed her a cup of tea.

"Why, yes of course. There are many gateways to other realms. The problem is finding the right one. We have had many visitors over the years that have come through the gateways. Some have been from this England."

"Do you know where they are and which one leads to England?" Carr was crushed at the hopeful look on her beautiful face. He wanted her to stay with them. To make a life here in Marak.

"No, no, no. There is no way to know when or where these gateways will appear. They are completely random. I'm sorry, girl. I wish I had more for you."

"What about the man that came from America and disappeared just before he was executed?" Carr asked. He remembered the story well, and though it was breaking his heart he wanted Jessica happy.

"That was true magic. The man opened a gateway right there in front of everyone. I have never seen anything like it. I spent years trying to figure out how it was done, but have been unsuccessful. These gateways are still a great puzzle and I'm afraid I might die and never know the answer."

"Can I look at your notes about the gateways? Maybe there is a pattern that you have missed." Jessica was tenacious. He'd give her that. She wasn't going to quit. Carr could picture the future. Married with three little babies at her feet and she still would be trying to find a gateway home. He smiled at the image. He really wanted to have babies with this woman. Would they have her blond hair and blue eyes or Baen's black hair and gray eyes?

He would have babies with her too, but he had to wait until Baen begot an heir. He could wait. He would still make love to her, but couldn't deposit his seed. That was all right. He knew the king's duty and respected that. As long as he was involved. His mind was getting away from him again. In his fantasy Carr had her wedded and bedded and she was still looking to leave them.

"All my notes are on that shelf there. You are welcome to them, but I have looked over and added to them for years and haven't discovered anything of use. You may very well be stuck here. You aren't the first and you won't be the last." Diarmad stood and shook an old pointy finger at Jessica. "My advice, young lady, is to make a life for yourself here. It will drive you mad otherwise. You have two great men offering you a life that others could only dream about. I would take it."

"Thank you, Diarmad. I will think about what you have said." Jessica shook the mage's hand and then went and grabbed the notes. Carr and Baen followed her out of the door and down the corridor. He grabbed her arm and swung her around to face him.

"I hope you weren't too disappointed with what the old man had to say," Carr said.

"Surprisingly, I'm not. I haven't given up, not yet, but I am getting used to the idea that my life may now be here." She smiled at him and his heart did a flip. She was so sweet and he wanted to feast on her. Baen moved in beside him and they backed her up against the castle wall.

He took her lips in a shattering kiss and pressed his body against her. Carr was tall, so he had to arch his back slightly to reach her. He needed to get her a pedestal that she could stand on when he kissed her. Otherwise he was going to get back problems.

He deepened the kiss and she moaned into his mouth. She tasted like tea and he tangled his tongue with hers, savoring the flavor. His cock was so hard in his pants, he wanted to lift her skirts and drive into her ready heat right there in the hallway.

Baen nudged his shoulder and he lifted his head. Passing her over to his lover, he cupped his erection and ran his hand up and down the length, then squeezed it to stop the impending orgasm. He didn't want to come in his pants like an untried boy, but watching his lover devour Jessica's lips was turning him on.

Baen lifted his head and let their woman go. She swayed on her feet and Carr reached out to steady her. She was just as affected by their kisses as they were. It gave him hope and he fully intended to use her passion against her. Baen and Carr couldn't make love to her until after the wedding, it was tradition, but they could do other things and he fully intended to take advantage of her weakness toward them.

Soon she would be putty in their hands and by the time the wedding day came around she would be begging for them to take her.

Chapter Seven

Jessica changed her gown and rushed out to meet Baen and Carr. They were taking her riding on Baen's dragon and she couldn't wait. Just being close to the dragon was enough to get her blood pumping with excitement, but to be able to ride on one was something she could have only dreamt about before coming to Marak.

The men had definitely brought out the big guns in their endeavor to woo her with this one. She had practically jumped on Baen when he had mentioned it. Then she had remembered herself and had politely accepted their offer. She wondered if she would ever stop embarrassing herself in front of them. She doubted it. She could get carried away sometimes.

She approached the stables at a jog after getting lost twice and having to ask for directions. The damned castle was so big she easily took a wrong turn and had to backtrack. She needed a map.

Baen and Carr were already there and had the horses ready. They had to ride out to meet the dragon Nughogg because he didn't like coming to close to the castle. She was going to ride on a gentle mare that was as old as the hills, but she didn't mind. Jessica wasn't very experienced with horses, so the gentler the better.

Carr helped lift her onto the horse and she adjusted her skirts. At least she didn't have to ride sidesaddle. The men would never have gotten her on the horse that way. The men mounted their stallions and they were off. She followed slowly behind, the mare plodding along at a steady pace.

They passed under the battlement and over the drawbridge. Jessica kept close to the men as they navigated their way around the market and out to the grassy field that separated the woods from the castle. Baen and Carr then kicked their horses into a gallop and raced across the open space.

Jessica's horse sped up to stay close to the men. She held onto the saddle tight as she bumped up and down and tried not to fall off. Once she got the hang of the horse's gait, she could relax and try to enjoy the ride.

When they reached the end of the field and were at the edge of the woods, the men pulled their horses to a stop and Jessica finally caught up and moved to follow. She was puffing slightly and her ass was already sore from banging against the hard leather of the saddle.

"Turn around and look, baby," Carr told her. "Isn't it a magnificent sight?"

Jessica swung her horse around to face back toward the castle. She sucked in a breath at the sight that greeted her. Carr was right, it was a magnificent view. The gray stone castle towered above a crystal blue lake, with a great wall wrapped around it for protection. The drawbridge was down and the marketplace was bustling with life.

Jessica wished she could take a photo. Something she could take back with her so she would never forget the sight, but she would have to be satisfied with the mental image instead. The castle looked so peaceful in its surroundings and she knew that was because Baen and Carr had fought year after year to keep it that way. The fighting and the constant battles all seemed worth it, in that moment. She could appreciate all that Baen and Carr had done and would have to do to preserve their way of life and keep the castle and its people safe.

It was then that she heard the strange sound that the dragon Knuckers had made when its wings flew through the sky. She watched in awe, as a huge black dragon flew over the top of the castle. It hovered in the sky, before starting its descent.

"It's the most beautiful thing I have ever seen. It makes me want to cry," she said, as tears threatened to spill from her eyes. It was hard to explain and she would never be able to put it into words, but the view of the pristine castle, with a dragon flying above it, had made her emotional. She wasn't sad. Far from it. The regal sight was just so overwhelming.

"You are the most beautiful thing I've ever seen, little one." Baen moved his horse in close and pulled her to him. She let out a yelp as she was lifted from one horse to another. He placed his mouth over hers and kissed her as if his life depended on it. As his lips moved over hers, she tried to convey the passion she felt in that moment.

Jessica moaned and sucked his bottom lip into her mouth, before letting go and tangling her tongue with his. They wrestled for control of the kiss, but Baen came out on top. He had moves that overpowered her and left her in a sensual fog. Her pussy dampened and she rubbed her legs together to soothe the ache.

It was getting serious, the need she had for these men. They had told her that they wouldn't take her until their wedding night, but in the meantime she was going insane. They kissed her, making love to her mouth, leaving her wanting and horny. Jessica was ready to jump Baen's bones right here on the horse.

"Come, you two. Nughogg is waiting." Carr's voice broke through her sensual fog. Baen lifted his head and smiled down at her.

"Are you ready for your ride, little one?" Baen asked her. She was, in more ways than one.

They slowly rode through the woods toward the dragon. Baen kept her on his lap and Carr pulled her mount along behind him. She had never ridden on someone's lap before, and it felt nice to be held.

They quickly made it through the woods and out the other side. Nughogg was waiting for them, his big wings folded against his massive body and his head down.

When Baen pulled to a stop, Jessica waited for Carr to come and help her down. He pulled her into his arms and gently lowered her to the ground. When her feet hit the ground, Nughogg let out a chuff and Jessica covered her ears with her hands.

"I think he likes you, baby," Carr said, chuckling. His smile was infectious and she found herself smiling back.

"What makes you say that?" Jessica couldn't see how that loud noise could mean that he liked her.

"Because you aren't roasted," Baen said from behind her. The men both laughed, but Jessica didn't get it.

"He's a fire dragon, baby. Nughogg can breathe fire from his mouth. When he feels threatened, smoke comes from his nostrils in warning." Carr's words didn't reassure her, but she did understand their joke. It was funny, if she thought about it, but their sense of humor was still lost on her.

"Come on, little one. Let's go meet Nughogg and go for that ride." Baen took her arm and they approached the dragon. He was amazing and a lot bigger than Knucker. Baen and Carr had explained to her that fire dragons grew a lot bigger than water dragons, which Knucker was.

Knucker lived in a lake and could breathe under water. He was like the Loch Ness monster and Jessica wondered if that was what it was, a dragon stuck in her realm and hiding in the Loch Ness.

The closer she got to him, the more differences she could see between the two dragons. Nughogg's black body shimmered in the light, like Knucker's, but he had bigger scales. His horns were in different places too. Knucker's were on his head and tail, but Nughogg just had ridges that ran the length of his spine and nothing on his head and tail.

Baen told her to wait at the dragon's side, as he scaled the big body to sit at the base of Nughogg's neck. He used the dragon's back feet and legs, which were resting next to his body, to climb up as if they were rocks. Then he walked along the body to his neck.

When he was settled, he gestured to Carr, who lifted her to stand on what would be the dragon's knee, before climbing up behind her. Jessica let out a squeak when the dragon shifted and she rocked forward with the movement. She quickly supported herself by placing her hand on the dragon's body. He was smooth under her hands. He felt a lot like a snake and Jessica ran her hands back and forth feeling his scales.

"Wow, this is amazing. I didn't think he would be so smooth. It's like silk. I thought he would feel more rubbery and rough," Jessica told Carr, as he stood behind her.

"I thought much the same when I first met him. He was smaller and younger then and a lot smoother." Carr grabbed her around the waist again and lifted her up and onto Nughogg's body. She used one of his back ridges to pull herself up and then held onto them, as she slowly made her way to Baen.

"Don't worry, Jessica. You can't hurt him," Baen said, and then pulled her down to sit on his lap. Carr sat down next to her and they were ready. There was no saddle like Elvinia used, and Jessica wondered why.

"Why did Elvinia use a saddle, but we aren't?" Jessica felt really unstable on the dragon despite the fact she was in Baen's arms. The huge dragon unfolded its massive wings and started to flap them up and down. The noise was a lot louder from here and she was tempted to cover her ears to block it out.

"Nughogg is much bigger, so it is easier to sit on him and not need one. You won't fall, Jessica, I won't let you." Baen's hot breath warmed her ear as he spoke softly into it. She shivered in response and leant further back into his arms. The higher the dragon climbed the scarier it became.

She was torn with emotions as the dragon flew through the sky. She was excited and fascinated about being able to ride such a magnificent creature, yet terrified and scared of falling at the same time. It was like being on a ride at a theme park and she had always hated those.

Nughogg didn't just fly in a straight line, he tucked and twirled and zoomed higher and lower. Baen and Carr looked thrilled with the ride. These two were certainly adrenaline junkies. When Jessica had the courage to open her eyes, she was impressed with the view and horrified at the height they were flying at.

Jessica could feel the wind ripple through her hair and because she had left it down it would be in a tangled mess when they returned. She pulled Baen's arms further around her middle and peeked out with one eye.

Nughogg's wings were open and motionless as they glided low over a lake. She heard the water ripple beneath his feet as he dipped his foot in the water below. His great wings flapped and they were rising again, as Knucker appeared beside them.

She let out a squeal as Knucker stretched out his long neck and nipped at the big black dragon's head. Nughogg chuffed and blew out a small fireball sending it Knucker's way. Knucker chuffed back and raced off, Nughogg hot on his tail.

Jessica buried her face in Baen's neck as the pace of the two dragons sped up. She heard Baen say something in her ear, but was too scared to find out what he had said. She felt the dragon slow, but not before he let out another loud chuff.

She had had enough now and couldn't wait to get back to solid ground. Jessica had had the experience of a lifetime, but she would be happy with the memory and even happier if she never had to get back on the big dragon again.

* * * *

Carr watched Jessica as she sat on Baen's lap. The poor thing's face was white as a sheet and she looked like she was going to throw up. He didn't blame her though. Dragon riding wasn't for everyone and Nughogg was showing off today. It didn't help that Knucker had decided to start a game of cat and mouse with him. Those two often mucked around, wrestling and chasing each other.

Baen had told Nughogg to stop and slow down. They wanted Jessica to enjoy the ride, not be terrified. She would never want to come again if she was scared, and Baen did so love to ride on his dragon. It was a good chance for them to get away from the pressures of royal life and just enjoy each other's company and their surroundings.

Carr leant over and brushed the hair back from Jessica's forehead. She opened her eyes at his touch and smiled over at him. Spirits, she was beautiful. Her blonde hair was wild and windswept around her head. Her little face, though pale, was flawless and her big blue eyes were wide.

He was losing his heart to the little minx, but he didn't mind. The more time he spent with her, the more he wanted her to stay with them forever. The wedding was fast approaching and he couldn't wait for the wedding night. They weren't going to make love to her until after the wedding, but they could do other stuff.

Kissing wasn't enough anymore. He wanted more and he didn't want to wait. He could tell she didn't either. The way she rubbed up against them when they kissed her was proof enough. He didn't see the point in waiting for the wedding night, but Baen had insisted. He was an old-fashioned man, and despite the fact that they knew she had been with men before Baen still wanted to wait.

So until then, he would settle himself with just tasting her delights. He wanted between those thighs, to the center of her womanhood. Then he would taste her flavor and lick her sweet cream until she screamed his name. Yes, there certainly were other things they could do to get to know each other better.

Carr didn't just want his mouth on her. He wanted her mouth on him too. To feel her soft lips around his cock, to slowly pump his length back and forth. How much of him would she be able to take?

Carr sighed and pulled himself back to the moment. His little baby wasn't enjoying her ride and so Carr gestured to Baen to get Nughogg to head home. With a couple of swift commands, they were making their way back toward the castle. They would have to find another way to woo their bride, because this wasn't working.

Maybe he would take her down to meet the kittens in the back of the stable. She mentioned something about a cat. Or maybe she would like to go on a picnic. Crap. What did he know of wooing women? He was a warrior, a fighter. All he knew was blood and death. Carr was a hard man and Baen was the only thing that had tamed him. Jessica was such a fragile little thing. Delicate and sweet. He needed to talk to Baen and see what ideas he had. Left to him, she would never want to stay.

It wasn't long before they were back at the field and Nughogg was folding his wings against his big body. He waited patiently as Baen and Carr helped Jessica to the ground, before he flew off. As he held Jessica, she was shaking in his arms and unstable on her feet.

Carr looked over at the horses to see Elvinia with two guards waiting for them. He walked Jessica over and mounted his horse before lifting her into his arms. She settled onto his lap and her color slowly returned.

"How was the ride? Wasn't it the most fun a person can have?" Elvinia asked. She had always loved riding the dragons and never had a problem with the height or speed. Poor Jessica. Elvinia would never understand her fears. She had been in the air on her dragon since Knucker was old enough to carry her.

"It was the most amazing experience of my life," Jessica replied. Carr was confused. He knew she hated it, it was written all over her face.

"Oh, I knew you would," Elvinia said, her excitement evident in the high pitch of her voice. "I can't wait to take—"

"I'm never going on the thing again and no one can make me. I shall enjoy its majestic presence from solid ground," Jessica cut in. Carr heard Baen's snort and Elvinia's indrawn breath.

"But you just said it was the most amazing experience of your life." Elvinia was confused and Carr couldn't blame her. Jessica was contradicting herself.

"It was amazing and terrifying and thrilling and scary and life-changing and horrible. I was so excited to go, but I never thought that once I was up there, I would spend the entire time waiting to plummet toward the ground. Nughogg was fast and all the twirling and twisting made me travel sick."

"Oh well, I guess." Elvinia's disappointment was evident in her tone.

"I'm sorry to disappoint you all. I really did try and enjoy it. I just couldn't."

"You could never disappoint us, little one. There are plenty more things that we can enjoy together and riding the dragon can be Carr's and my special thing," Baen told her. Carr couldn't have put it better himself. Besides, he still had a few tricks up his sleeve.

They all rode back toward the castle, Jessica snug in Carr's arms. She snuggled into him and he tightened his arms around her, placing a kiss to her forehead.

* * * *

Jessica walked back to her room in a daze. She was still stunned from her ride on a real-life dragon. It had been exhilarating and terrifying at the same time and she never wanted to repeat the experience.

She opened the heavy door to her chambers and quietly shut it behind her. With three quick strides she was at the bed. She flopped down face-first and lay there contemplating her next move.

The more time she spent with her men the more she cared for them and slowly, little by little, her resistance was wavering. They were funny, charming, strong, and dominant. Everything she had ever looked for in man, or men in this case. She was doomed.

Jessica knew that she had to find a way out of this realm and back to her own. Falling for the men was just going to leave her heart broken and alone. Why had she ever agreed to their crazy idea of marriage?

The wedding was fast approaching. She knew once she let them have her body, they would have her heart as well. She wasn't someone that rushed into sex lightly and these men were sex on a stick.

If she did find a way home, that meant she would be able to find a way back again. Maybe she just needed to go home and tie up a few loose ends. Then she would be free to come back and pick up where she left off.

Oh, who was she kidding. They were just marrying her for protection. Yes, they had been sweet and kind and attentive, but that was just because they wanted her to feel welcome, not because they wanted her forever.

No, she had to harden her heart and remember that, she was a strong independent woman. One who had a fulfilling and rich life back in her own realm. A realm that had no magic and no dragons and no big dominant men, who drove her crazy and made her want to throw herself at them at the same time.

Jessica rolled onto her back and stared at the ceiling, sighing loudly. She would just try to avoid them as much as possible until she found a way home. No more romantic rides and no more canoodling in the hallways.

Then again, she loved the canoodling. Jessica closed her eyes, her thoughts drifting and a smile on her face.

Chapter Eight

Jessica sat in her chamber and pored over the notes that she got from Diarmad. It was her wedding day, but she wasn't giving up. Diarmad's notes were extensive, but he was right, there was no discernable pattern. It was completely random and the gateways led to a number of realms other than hers. The thought was staggering. Most people thought that only one Earth existed, not multiple realms. They were all Earth, but different. They all had similarities, but none were the same.

She had noticed that here in Marak. It was very similar to medieval England, as far as she could see. She really could only compare it to the history books she read. Jessica wondered what had created the different realms and why they were all moving at a different pace. Were some more advanced than her Earth? She had to assume that was the case.

She looked up from the notes when the door opened and Elvinia walked into the room. She was carrying a white dress, which she gently placed on the bed next to her. Crap, was that her wedding dress? It was absolutely gorgeous. The floor-length gown was the same style as the ones she had been wearing, but this was so much more elegant and refined. Solid white, it had gold trimming that bordered the sleeves and the panel at the front. It tied up with a gold cord and had a gold chain-link belt.

"Time to get ready, Jessica. To think that in just over an hour, we will be sisters." Elvinia smiled and flapped her hand excitedly as she spoke. Jessica was glad that she was so welcome into the family. She had met Baen's mother, a few days past, and she had been lovely. She remembered the meeting well.

Fenella was a regal woman. She was tall, thin, and had Baen's black hair and Elvinia's violet eyes. Softly spoken, she commanded the room with grace and charm. Meeting the soon-to-be mother-in-law was a frightening experience in any case, but meeting the queen mother was especially scary. Luckily for Jessica, she warmly welcomed her into the family and made her feel right at ease in her presence.

"Well, hello there, my dear," the queen mother said. "I have been eagerly waiting to meet you. Baen has told me such wonderful things."

Fenella took Jessica's hand in her own and gave it a gentle squeeze.

"Hello, it's such a pleasure to meet you too," Jessica replied. She wished that Baen and Carr were here with her, but they were off doing royal duties and she had been left to meet the queen mother with Elvinia for support.

"Come, sit. We shall have some tea and you can tell me a little about yourself." Jessica walked over and watched Fenella and Elvinia delicately perch on the ends of their seats. They made Jessica feel like a bull in a china shop and, with a sigh that could be heard clear across the room, she plopped down in her seat and tried not to embarrass herself to much.

"Mother," Elvinia said. "I thought Jessica was going to pass out, when she got of the Nughogg, the other week. You should have seen her face. She was practically green."

Jessica's eyes snapped over to the queen mother. Fenella was chuckling behind her hand, tears pouring from her eyes. Jessica stared at her in shock. Her mouth flapped open and shut, but no words came out, as Fenella continued to laugh.

"I'm sorry, my dear. I really am. It was rude of me to laugh at you."

"Mother," Elvinia said. "I can't see why you're in such hysterics. You hate flying on the dragons just as much."

This made Fenella laugh all the more and just like that the tension drained from Jessica's body. She didn't understand what was so funny and she didn't really care. It had made Fenella more human and less of the queen mother.

The three women spent the rest of the afternoon drinking tea and talking. Fenella told Jessica tales from when Baen and Carr were boys and even managed to embarrass Elvinia a time or two.

When Jessica finally left the queen mother's chambers, she had felt a sense of belonging and friendship. She had missed that growing up and it had made her doubt her determination to find a way home.

"Is it that time already?" Jessica was shocked. Where had the day gone? It wasn't the first time she had lost herself in Diarmad's notes. She had missed a few meals because she was distracted. It annoyed Baen and Carr to no end.

"There you are," Carr said. "We have been waiting for you in the hall. I thought you had gotten lost again."

Jessica looked up from her notes and smiled at the disgruntled look on Carr's face. Oops, she had done it again. She was supposed to meet with Baen and Carr in the hall for the noon meal.

"I'm sorry," she replied. "I lost track of time and there was this really good note about a man who came through the veil and—."

"No more, Jessica." Carr was getting angry. The more she spoke about Diarmad's notes, the angrier the men got. She didn't want to upset them, but it was fascinating to read and she got swept up in the excitement of it all. Diarmad was a great storyteller and his details were so descriptive.

"I'm sorry, Carr. I won't let it happen again."

"Don't, or Baen won't be the only one threatening to put you over his knee and spank you," Carr told her.

Baen had threatened her with a spanking last time she had stood them up. The idea had intrigued her and frightened her at the same time. Jessica sighed and followed Carr to the hall. She was getting hungry now that she wasn't distracted by the notes. Carr's threat had made her hungry for more than just food and she wondered if she could tempt them into fooling around with her a little.

A cough brought her back to the present. Jessica put the notes aside and stood. She removed her gown, but left on her chemise. Elvinia helped her put the elegant gown over her head and slip her arms through the long sleeves. Then she tied the cord between her breasts and adjusted the gold chain belt, so it angled just so on her hips.

She wished that she could see herself in the mirror, but hadn't seen one around. There didn't appear to be a mirror in the whole damned castle. She hoped she looked all right. Why was she stressing? It was just her wedding day to two of the most stunning specimens of men to ever walk the Earth. In her realm and this one.

Elvinia gestured for her to sit on a chair. She started to brush out Jessica's wild locks. She had washed it that morning so it was in tight ringlets that fell uncontrollably around her head. She had never been able to tame her hair and so she had given up trying and just let it run wild. The look suited her and so she just left it.

"You look beautiful. Baen and Carr are going to swoon when they see you," Elvinia said as she placed a small gold tiara in her hair and pinned it into place.

"Thank you. I appreciate the help. Could you please give me a few moments alone?" She wanted to catch her breath and maybe freak out a little about the enormity of what she was about to do.

"Sure. Mother will come and get you when it is time. She wants to escort you to my brother. She said that because you had no family present, she would take that role."

"That's fine. Thank you." Jessica watched as Elvinia left the room and then let out a huge breath. She was getting married. It was crazy and scary and so exciting she thought she was going to throw up.

Jessica still thought that marrying Baen and Carr for protection was a silly idea, and even though she had come to care for them deeply she was still trying to find a way home. It wasn't their fault, not at all. They had done everything possible to make her feel cared for and wanted. It was just that she felt that if she didn't try and get home, she would always wonder.

Yet again, here she was standing in her wedding dress and about to walk down the aisle. She understood that she might never find a way to get back to her realm. She was slowly starting to accept that. Baen and Carr were making it easy for her. Every time she was with them, her heart raced and all she could think about was how sexy they were and how good they would be in the bedroom.

She would find out tonight, that was certain, and she couldn't wait. Making love with them both was going to blow her mind. Jessica was even turned on by the idea of them making love to each other. She wanted to watch and maybe participate in some way.

God, what the hell was she thinking? Her mind was going from one thing to another and she was about to explode. She was going, she was staying, she shouldn't marry, she should marry. She wanted sex and, well, she just wanted sex. At least she was sure about that.

There was a knock at the door and Fenella entered the chamber. She looked stunning in her dark blue gown with silver trimming. Her black hair was pulled away from her face and she was wearing a small crown that had three large sapphires on the front. Jessica stood and fidgeted her hands together as she waited for the queen mother to approach.

"You look beautiful, my dear. My son and his consort are lucky men." Fenella took her hand as she spoke and gave it a gentle squeeze. Jessica tilted her head in confusion.

"You know that Baen and Carr are lovers?" she asked. She didn't realize how open the men's relationship was.

"Of course. My son has always been open about his love for the commander of his armies," the queen mother replied. Jessica was amazed.

"And no one cares that the king has a same-sex lover?"

"No, why should they? Marak has always been very open and accepting about relations between same-gender couples. Our society is built on this acceptance. My husband, rest his soul, fought his entire reign to give his people a safe haven where they can live openly and honestly."

"That is amazing. In my Earth, while being gay is mostly accepted, it is still a long way from being truly the norm. Lots of countries don't allow same-sex marriages and there are a lot of people who openly shun the gay community."

"Love is love, my dear. My son isn't a lesser king because he loves another man. He is stronger for it. Only narrow-minded people would think differently." The queen mother was a knowledgeable woman. If only the leaders of her Earth were so free thinking.

They walked from the chamber and made their way toward the great hall where the ceremony was to take place. Jessica was quiet for most of the walk, but Fenella chattered away about one thing or another. By the time they had reached the great hall, Jessica was a bundle of nerves. Her stomach was doing somersaults and there was a very good chance she was going to throw up.

"It's all right, dear. I was nervous on my wedding day too. Come see me after and we will discuss the wedding night." Fenella patted her hand and smiled down at her. Jessica stared. She didn't know what to say. Her soon-to-be mother-in-law wanted to have the "birds and the bees" talk. She nodded her head and tried to smile in return. It wasn't the queen mother's business that she wasn't a virgin. Nor was it the right time to tell her.

The doors to the great hall opened and Jessica and the queen mother made their way down the long aisle. Jessica looked around to avoid looking at the faces of the crowd that filled the room. There were flowers hanging in large arches from the ceiling and white material with gold trim hung in panels on the walls. Large candelabras were scattered around the room and lit fires warmed the chilly air. A long bottle-green rug ran the length of the great hall and led her to her men.

Jessica reached Baen and Carr quickly. Fenella passed her over to them and then took her place in the front row next to Elvinia. A man in long robes stood before them. He said a few words she didn't understand, which could have been Latin, before switching to English.

Jessica studied the man as he spoke of love and friendship. He looked like a priest, but Jessica saw no crosses and he spoke no words about God or Jesus. His long bottle-green robes went all the way to his feet and he wore a floppy cap on his head. He had long gray hair and was a man well into his later years.

He went on to talk about commitment and honoring your loved ones, but it wasn't until he spoke of marriage between all three of them that Jessica started to pay attention.

"We are brought here today to witness the commitment of Baen to Jessica, Jessica to Carr, and Baen and Carr to each other." Eh? If that wasn't confusing she didn't know what was. "Love is a most sacred thing. When we find that love, we must fight to hold it. We must nurture it and keep it safe and let no one steal it away."

As the celebrant went on and on about love and its spiritual connection, Jessica looked over at her men. They looked hot in their matching wedding attire. Their white sleeveless shirts had the same gold trim and laced cords as her dress. Their black breeches were molded to their strong, muscled thighs. Knee-high boots polished to a shine finished off their outfits. The only difference between them was Baen wore a floor-length white cape and a large jeweled crown. Jessica assumed this was because he was the king.

They were so good-looking. It was overwhelming standing in their presence. They made a striking couple and Jessica couldn't wait until she got them alone. Thoughts she really shouldn't be having in the middle of her wedding ceremony. She could feel herself blush and looked down toward her hands.

The celebrant brought her attention back to the ceremony, asking them to exchange their vows. Baen went first, promising to love and protect her and Carr, and always put their needs before others. Carr went next, and though he offered up the same, he added that he would always do right by Baen and the monarchy. Then it was Jessica's turn.

She stood up straight and looked up at her men. The men who would be her husbands and her entire world if she let them. Maybe she should have written her vows before it was time to say them. Crap. She felt her palms getting sweaty, as Baen and Carr stood there patiently and waited for her to speak.

"Baen and Carr, I want to be with you just as you are. I choose you above all others, to share my life. I love you for your strengths and your weakness and will stand by you, as you become all you can be. I promise to be true and faithful to you and the people of Marak. I promise to honor this pledge as long as I live." Jessica let out a breath in a rush. She hoped that was good enough.

When they reached the part where people normally exchanged rings, the celebrant stopped. He picked up a white cape, which was the same as the one that Baen wore, and placed it on Carr's shoulders, and then he did the same to her. The cape felt heavy on her shoulders and she wondered about its significance. It had to have something to do with Baen being the king.

The celebrant then asked them to kneel. Baen knelt in the middle with Carr on his left and Jessica on his right. The queen mother approached with a pair of servants holding two crowns on dark green cushions. She approached Carr first and held the crown high above his head.

"Carr, you have given your vow on this day and pledged yourself to the king and his people. From this day forth, let no man come between you. As the king's consort, you will lead in his absence. May the spirits be with you and guide you on your journey." Fenella put the crown on his head and walked over to her. She lifted a thin version of the crown Baen and Carr wore and held it above her head.

"Jessica, you have given your vow on this day and pledged yourself to the king, consort, and their people. From this day forth, let no man come between you. As Queen, you will love, cherish and guide the kingdom toward a better future. May the spirits make you fertile and guide you on your journey." Jessica felt the weight of the crown settle on her head. It was a huge responsibility. She was the queen to a kingdom of people she knew nothing about.

Jessica rose as Baen pulled her to her feet. The celebrant turned them toward the crowd and presented them as husband, husband, and wife. Baen swept her up in his arms and kissed her. He stole her breath and left her standing there panting as he turned and did the same to Carr. It was then Carr's turn to kiss her. He spun her around and lifted her off her feet. She felt his tongue probe the cavern of her mouth before she was gently placed down back onto her feet.

Baen strode down the aisle dragging her and Carr behind him. The crowd roared and cheered as they strode from the room.

"Slow down, Baen. My legs aren't as long as yours." Jessica was almost running to keep up with him. Baen didn't slow down. He simply swept her up into his powerful arms and kept on going. Jessica didn't know what the rush was. Nor did she know where they were headed. Wherever it was, Baen wanted to get there in all possible haste.

Jessica put her arms around her new husband's neck and held on. She was so far off the ground. The man was really tall. She clung on to his neck and looked at him as he walked. She was married to this fine man. It was mind-boggling. He looked every bit the powerful king, as he strode through the castle in his cape and crown. She had walked through the veil simply to see what was on the other side and now she was married and the queen.

She looked away from Baen and over his shoulder to Carr. He strode behind Baen with determination. His strong body moved with grace. He was a warrior through and through. From his strong, chiseled body to his hard, scarred face. He was magnificent and he was hers. She smiled at the thought. They both were hers and she couldn't wait to get them naked.

* * * *

Baen kicked the door to his chambers open and strode into the room. Jessica felt so small and fragile in his arms, but felt so right. He was reluctant to put her down. He wanted to hold her all night. He gently placed her on the bed and stood back to look at her. God, she was beautiful. Her big blue eyes looked up at him and he could see her confusion.

"Why are we here?" she asked. Jessica tried to get off the bed, but he was having none of it. He gently pushed her back down, before taking one of her feet in his hand.

"If you have to ask that, I should have let my mother give you the talk." Baen heard Carr laugh at his joke, but his little queen just looked more confused. He removed one of her slippers and then swapped feet to remove the other.

"What about the reception? Your mother has been talking about it for weeks." She slapped his hands away as he tried to remove her gold belt.

"They will have the reception without us, baby," Carr said behind him. "We have more important matters to see to. Like begetting an heir for the kingdom."

"I was thinking more along the lines of making love to my new wife and husband," Baen rebuked. "We can beget heirs tomorrow." This was their wedding night. He didn't want either of them to worry about their royal duty. This night was about them and cementing their bond of matrimony.

"Stop slapping my hands away, little one. I'm trying to remove your garments," he told her.

"I know, that's why I'm doing it. I can get undressed myself."

"Yes, but it's much more fun if I do it." Baen untied her laces at the front of her gown and loosened them. Then he lifted the heavy gown over her head and threw it behind him. Carr moved to lie on the bed next to Jessica. He had removed his boots and cape and lay there in his breeches and tunic.

He looked back at Jessica in only her chemise. It was so thin her dark pink nipples could be seen through the material. They pebbled under his inspection, and he reached out and pinched one gently between his finger and thumb. She sucked in a breath, but didn't say anything.

He watched as Carr leant over and took her mouth in a passion-filled kiss. He had loved Carr for so long his heart was full to bursting. He didn't think he could ever love another the way he did Carr. But a little slip of a woman with bouncy blonde hair and big blue eyes was pushing her way into his heart and there was nothing he could do to stop it. Not that he wanted to. He had more than enough love to give and now was the time to prove it.

He removed his boots and cape, and then placed his crown on the table before returning to his lovers. He stripped naked and stood at the end of the bed in all his glory. His cock was hard and pointing straight at his lovers. He reached down and stroked it as he waited for his wife and husband to notice him.

It wasn't long before Carr broke their kiss and looked over at him.

"It's about time you two came up for air. The king needs loving too," he told them. He saw Jessica's eyes flare when she took in the size of his throbbing cock. He wasn't a little man in any department. Carr often praised him on the size of his manhood.

"Get our baby naked, Carr. I want to see her."

"You don't mean to come anywhere near me with that thing, do you?" Jessica asked. Her voice was high pitched and shaky. He smiled at her and stroked it once more.

"Don't worry, little one. It will fit. You were made for Carr and me. We will make sure you are ready." Jessica was pushing Carr away as he tried to strip her of her chemise. This wasn't how he saw this night progressing, but he could turn it around. He gently shoved Carr out of the way and grabbed the bottom of her chemise and pulled it over her head. She covered her breasts with her hands and crossed her legs to hide her feminine parts.

"Don't hide from us, little one. You are very beautiful and we want to see all of you. Carr, get naked, it might make her more comfortable."

"If he's hung like you, I doubt it." Sassy little thing, she was. Baen didn't care. He thought she was funny. He moved onto the bed next to her and peeled her hands away from her breasts. They were high and firm and had large, dark-pink nipples. His mouth watered at the sight and Baen could do none other than take one into his mouth and gently bite down.

Once Carr was naked, he moved up the bed and grabbed her legs. He had to use a bit of pressure to get her to open her thighs, but after some persuasion, she parted her legs. Carr nudged her thigh wider with his shoulders as he settled on his belly in between.

"God, baby. You have a gorgeous pussy. So pink and wet. I have to taste it." Carr ducked his head and Baen heard Jessica gasp. She liked what Carr was doing to her. Her chest started to rise and fall rapidly.

"Do you like that, little girl? Do you like Carr licking your sweet pussy?" Baen spoke the words softly in her ear and watched her head nod the affirmative.

"You have to try her, Baen. She tastes so fucking good. Like a spring morning, fresh and floral."

"I'll get my turn. I'm playing with these fine twin mounds." Baen took her breast in his mouth again and suckled at the nipple. He pinched and rolled the other nipple between his fingers. Soon Jessica was moaning and thrashing beneath them. He raised his head from her breast and took her mouth in a kiss. Her lips were soft and yielding under his masterful touch. Their tongues danced together, thrusting and parrying.

Baen's heart beat rapidly in his chest and his cock throbbed and leaked clear fluid onto his thigh. He couldn't wait to get inside her warm heat and hoped he didn't disgrace himself by coming the moment he entered her.

Jessica shuddered beneath him and he caught her scream in his mouth. Carr had done a good job of bringing their little wife to orgasm, but it wasn't finished yet.

"My turn, lover. Can't let you have all the fun." Baen shoved Carr out of the way and took up position between Jessica's parted thighs. "You weren't wrong, lover. She does have a beautiful pussy." He ran his thumb up and over her little bud and watched her moan and thrust her hips. Her pussy juices coated his thumb. She was so wet from her previous orgasm. He leaned his head closer and ran his tongue from the bottom of her pussy to her clit, licking up her juices. She tasted fine. Spicy and sweet and all Jessica. He would never get tired of her flavor.

"Open up, baby. Take me in your mouth." Carr knelt on the bed, holding out his long cock to Jessica. Baen watched over the top of her body as she opened her mouth and took the mushroom-shaped head between her lips. Carr threw his head back and moaned as she licked his slit and swirled her tongue.

Baen thought it was the hottest thing he ever saw. His little wife sucking his husband's cock and tonguing the little eye. Fuck, if he watched anymore he was doomed. He got back to licking her dripping pussy and slipped a finger inside her tight hole. She was small. It was going to take some doing to get his large cock inside.

He added another finger and scissored them in and out as he ran his tongue back and forth over her throbbing clit. Her juices ran over his fingers and eased his way. It wasn't long before she was thrusting her hips up at him. Baen added another finger and rammed them into her waiting hole. He could just make out her moans of desire as she sucked his lover's long length.

When she exploded under his tongue, he felt her pussy muscles contract around his probing fingers. He slowly brought her back down and then lifted his head. She was still attached to Carr, her head bobbing as she worked his cock between her lips.

Baen moved up her delectable body and placed the head of his cock at the entrance to her pussy. He slowly started to push forward, her warm heat engulfing him in a tight fist.

"Fuck, little one. You are so fucking tight. You are going to squeeze my cock to death." He panted and moaned as he entered her little by little. If this wasn't pure torture, he didn't know what was. She was so hot he was going to lose his load before he worked his whole length inside her.

Baen dropped his head to his chest and pushed forward. Not much more and he would be fully seated inside her. She shifted her hips under him, lifting them closer and forcing more of his cock into her channel.

"Baen, please. It feels so good. Your cock is so big, I don't think I can take much more." She lifted her head only long enough to speak and then took Carr back between her lips.

"Not much more, baby girl. I'm almost there." Baen froze when he had worked his large cock all the way inside her.

"Oh, baby. Your mouth is so hot. It feels so good. You have to stop, I'm going to come." Carr was thrusting his hips back and forth and groaning. Baen watched as Carr gritted his teeth and tried not to come. "Baby, I mean it. If you don't stop now, I'm going to come. So unless you want me to finish in your mouth, I'd let go."

Jessica wasn't having any of it. She took his cock in her hand and kept on sucking. When Carr threw his head back and roared, Baen almost came along with him. He had to squeeze the end of his dick to stop himself from filling her tight pussy with his seed.

When she finally lifted her head, he watched as Carr slumped onto the bed beside her. She smiled up at him and held open her arms.

"Come here, Baen, and make love to me. I need to feel you move." That was an offer Baen couldn't refuse. He leaned down until his chest touched hers and slowly pumped his hip back and forth. He had to clench his jaw she was so damned hot and tight.

"You're so hot, little one. I could live here inside your tight little pussy." He leant forward and took her lips in his. He nipped at her bottom lip as he worked his cock in and out.

"Stop teasing me, Baen. Fuck me already." Baen paused his strokes. Jessica had taken him by surprise. He had never had such a forceful woman in the bedroom and never one that used such language. It turned him on, but he would show her who was boss in the bedchamber.

"You want me to fuck you, do you, little girl? Then you need to ask nicely. Beg me to fuck you. Beg me to take you and make you mine." He resumed his slow torturous pace, as Jessica wiggled and shifted beneath him.

"Please, Baen. Please fuck me. Please, I beg you."

"Now that's better." He picked up his pace and thrust his length into her waiting heat. Again and again he moved back and forth, until they were both panting and moaning, desperate for release.

"Help her out, Carr." Baen moved back slightly to give Carr room. He felt his lover's hand move between their bodies and rub against her little bud. Jessica groaned again, and he knew she was near completion.

It only took another couple of hard thrusts and Jessica screamed out her orgasm below him, her pussy squeezing his cock. He followed her over, roaring as his release shot through his body and exploded out of his cock. Streams of his life's essence filled her waiting pussy, as he shook above her.

Carr reached over and placed a hand on the back of his neck, as he tried to keep his weight from crushing Jessica. She had wrung him dry and he was drained of energy. It had been an Earth-shattering explosion, but he would only need a few minutes before they could do it again.

"Wow, just wow." Jessica spoke from under him. Baen let out a little chuckle. His thoughts exactly.

Chapter Nine

Jessica lay on the bed completely naked and exposed to her new husbands' gazes. She watched them as they moved around the room, tidying and cleaning themselves up. They had taken care of her first, gently washing away the evidence of their lovemaking and assuring themselves that she wasn't damaged in any way.

She had blushed through their inspection and tried to shove them away. Baen had slapped her on her thigh and demanded that she hold still and let them care for her. Who was she to deny them that simple pleasure? If they wanted to pamper her after sex, she was just going to have to let them.

And what amazing sex it had been. She never knew it could be that good. It had rocked her world. It was true that she didn't have much experience with men. Most thought she was odd. But what they had just done was so out of anything she had come close to experiencing.

They both gave her the most incredible orgasms when they licked her pussy. She had finished twice before Baen had entered her. They had astounding tongues. She could have kept them at it all night. When they had kissed her and she had tasted herself on their lips, she was turned on even more.

She had even enjoyed giving Carr a blowjob. Normally she suffered through it and couldn't wait for it to be over. But with Carr, she felt excited to have the power to bring him pleasure. It had turned her on. She wanted to taste him on her tongue when he came in her mouth.

Then there was Baen. He had a monster-sized cock she didn't think was going to fit. He did, and they had made sure she was good and ready before entering her. He had touched places inside her that no one had before. She was ruined for all other men. No one would compare to their lovemaking.

The worst part was she was ready for more. Baen and Carr looked like they were finished, but she wanted to go again. They had turned her into a wanton. She was going to become a sex-crazed addict. The men wouldn't get any rest. Jessica giggled to herself and the men looked over. One bout of mind-blowing sex and she had lost her mind.

"What has you giggling, little one?" Baen asked. He stood at the end of the bed completely naked with his hands on his hips.

"Oh, I was just thinking silly thoughts. But surely we aren't finished? Is that it? Have I wrung you out already? I thought the king and his commander would have more stamina." Jessica smiled a sassy smile their way. She shifted on the bed to lie on her side and placed her head in her palm. She hoped it was a sexy pose. She wanted to entice the men back into bed and get them to make love to her again.

"You are pushing your luck, little girl. We were trying to give you time to recover. We are big men and didn't want you hurting."

"I'm stronger than I look, Baen. You left me wanting. Now get over here and do your husbandly duties."

"Carr, get the grease. Our sassy little Queen wants to play."

"She is certainly asking for trouble, my lover. Let's show our baby who the masters of the bedchamber are," Carr added. He grabbed something from a shelf and returned to the bed.

Jessica admired their form as they both approached her. They were big men and made her feel so small next to them. Naked, they were a force to be reckoned with. They took her breath away, and little by little they were stealing her heart.

"On your hands and knees, little girl. Head down, rear up. I want access to what's mine." She did what she was told, and Baen moved in behind her. Carr moved to lie at her side. Jessica laid her head on the bed and looked at Carr. They stared into each other's eyes and she felt a connection flow between them. She had never felt this close and in touch with another human being, let alone a man. The more time she spent with them, the more she wanted to stay.

Her attention was brought back to Baen when she felt a hard slap to her rear. She let out a small gasp in shock, but didn't protest. It had felt good and she wanted him to do it again.

"Our baby liked that, Baen. Her eyes just darkened and her breath went choppy. I think you should do it again." Carr was talking to Baen, but he was looking at her. He wore a smug smile on his handsome, scarred face.

Baen smacked her ass a few more times and Jessica groaned as the sting turned into heat. That heat went straight to her pussy and it throbbed and demanded attention.

She had never been smacked before, not even by her parents as a child. It was turning her on and Jessica could tell it was turning her men on as well.

"Baen likes to smack, baby. Now that he has you my ass might get a rest." Carr's smile was wide and cheeky. Jessica's heart melted more.

"Not a chance, my love. I will never tire of reddening your firm cheeks." Wow, Jessica had married two kinky men. Not that she minded. It was consensual and in good fun. "Hold still, little girl. I'm going to stretch out your little hole. Have you ever had anything in your ass before?"

"No, I haven't tried it before. It's not going to hurt, is it?" Jessica was concerned. She had never had anal before, though she knew that a lot of people did.

"Don't worry, baby. Baen will take good care of you. It will sting and burn at first, but we would never cause you pain. If you don't like it or it hurts, just tell us to stop and we will." Carr brushed the hair back on her forehead as he spoke. His reassurance calmed her nerves.

"Ok, I'm ready. I trust you both."

Jessica felt Baen circle her back passage with his finger, spreading grease around as he went. It felt good. Jessica sighed and squirmed around impatiently. She wasn't kept waiting long. Baen slid one long finger inside.

"Oh, I didn't realize. It feels good, strange but good," Jessica told them. She heard the men chuckle behind her. This was uncharted territory they were playing in. Jessica wasn't in the mood for games. "Just get to it."

The slap on her ass was unexpected and made her draw in a breath.

"We will do this at my pace, little girl. Settle down and try to enjoy it." Baen was working his finger in and out of her hole. When he finally added another finger and started to scissor them in and out, Jessica thought she was going to come. The tight burning sensation made her squirm away from his touch, but the pleasure it morphed into made her squirm closer. She was in a world of conflicting emotions and all her nerve endings were alive.

Jessica felt empty when Baen stopped and removed his fingers. She didn't want him to stop and moaned her displeasure.

"Climb onto Carr, little one, and take him into your pussy." Jessica moved to straddle Carr and did as Baen told her to. As she sank down onto Carr's hard length, he groaned. She moved her hips up and down, working his cock inside her tight wet channel and grinding her clit onto his pelvis. When she finally had him all the way to the hilt, she was panting and desperately trying not to orgasm.

"All right, little one. Relax your muscles and let me in." Baen gently pushed her down onto Carr's chest and lined his cock up with her tight back entrance. He pushed at the muscle and Jessica drew in a sharp breath at the burning pain that engulfed her.

"Oh God, Baen. I can't. You're too big." She tried to pull away but Carr's hands on her hips easily held her in place.

"Shh, baby. It's all right, relax and push back. Baen won't hurt you, he will fit." Carr leaned into her and took her lips. The kiss had her stomach doing somersaults and her pussy clenching around his cock. It also distracted her from Baen and with a pop he pushed the mushroom head of his cock through her tight ring of muscle.

"I'm in, little one. You feel amazing. So tight and hot. I can feel Carr through the thin muscle separating us." Baen started to move his length forward and back, Carr soon following. As one moved forward, the other moved out and vice versa. Jessica was overwhelmed by the sensations. She wiggled and bucked between them, working her body in time with her lovers.

"That feels so good. Like nothing I've ever felt before. I need more, please move faster." Jessica loved the feel of her men as they rode her, one filling her pussy and the other in her ass. She never expected to like having her back passage filled, but Baen and Carr had opened her eyes to another sexual experience and she was so thankful that she trusted them to take care of her.

"That's it baby, ride my cock. I want to feel that sweet pussy tighten around me when you come." Carr slammed into her, his big hands on her hips. Baen reached around and cupped her breasts, squeezing and massaging as he fucked her ass with abandon.

"Fuck yes. You feel so good. God, Carr, she's so tight. She is squeezing my cock so fucking hard." Baen and Carr sure liked to talk while making love. She had never had such talkative lovers before. They just didn't shut up and it turned her on more. It made her feel powerful and sexy to know that she affected them this much.

"Oh, I'm going to come. I'm so close." Jessica threw her head back and moaned to the ceiling. Her orgasm was building and she knew it was going to be epic.

"That's it, baby. Let loose and come all over my cock." With Carr's words ringing in her ears, Jessica screamed out her release. It started deep in her stomach and spread through her body, shooting through her pussy until she was a spent and quivering mass of feeling.

It wasn't long until Baen grabbed her hips and pounded into her once, twice, and then he roared his release, shooting his cum into her back passage. This spurred Carr on and soon he too was driving his cock into her pussy and slamming her hips down toward him.

Baen slowly pulled his spent cock from her ass and Carr rolled them over until she lay beneath him. He took her mouth in a ravenous kiss and hooked her legs over his arms. He continued to pound into her and she was soon close to orgasm once more. She didn't know how they did it, but they worked her body like a finely tuned machine and she was powerless to stop it.

She ripped her mouth from Carr's as another powerful explosion raked her body. Jessica arched her back off the bed and ground her clit against Carr as her orgasm went on and on. She slumped down onto the bed below, drained and wrung out. Carr pulled his still hard cock from her dripping pussy and, taking it in hand, pumped it back and forth before shooting his seed onto her stomach. He dropped his head down as he groaned out his release before collapsing on top of her.

Jessica loved the weight and feel of her big warrior slumped on top of her. She ran her hands over his back and down toward his tight ass. She felt him shiver beneath her light touch. She grew bolder in her explorations and took each of his ass checks in her hands and squeezed.

"Baby, as much as I'd love to make love to you again, I'm going to need a little longer to recover." Carr's voice was gruff with weariness. He rolled off her and flopped onto the bed beside her. Baen moved in with a cloth and cleaned her, wiping away Carr's seed.

"You have to give him some rest, little one. He isn't as young as he used to be." Baen was chuckling as he spoke and Carr lifted his hand to flip him off. It appeared the bird was a universal gesture no matter what realm you were in.

"You can talk, you are older than I am," Carr added.

"By two years at most, old man," Baen said, as he wrapped her up in the blankets and then crawled in beside her. "I have more than enough stamina to satisfy our little queen, as much as she needs."

"Easy to say that when our baby is asleep."

"I'm not asleep, not yet anyway. We can go again." Jessica tried not to laugh. She really just wanted to go to sleep, but couldn't help joining in on the teasing.

"Oh God, you're going to kill me." Baen groaned, and Carr laughed. She loved the easy banter and the way they felt comfortable enough to tease each other. This was how a relationship was meant to be. It wasn't conventional, and back on her Earth it wouldn't be accepted, but here they could be themselves. For the first time, Jessica felt like she belonged and she knew she had made the right decision in marrying Baen and Carr. Well, technically she was told she was marrying them, but she could have put up more of a fight.

They all snuggled into the big bed together, Baen spooning her from behind and Carr holding her close to his front. Jessica closed her eyes and let sleep take her. She still wasn't sure what the future would bring, but with her two new husbands at her side, Jessica knew that it wasn't going to be mundane, and that each day was going to be an adventure in itself.

* * * *

Carr was restless. He couldn't sleep, and his cock was hard again. It was still the middle of the night and he had woken with Jessica's ass pressed against his erection. He was grinding into her before he was fully awake and aware of what he was doing. Now he was wide-awake and his two lovers were dead to the world.

Carr rolled onto his back and decided to take the matter in hand. Grasping his long cock in his fist, he slowly pumped back and forth. He had to stifle a moan as he worked his cock.

"Need any help with that?" Jessica surprised him. Carr had thought she was asleep. She sat up and straddled his thighs, knocking his hand away and taking his cock in her own. She was shy and hesitant as she tried to jerk him off, her innocence endearing, and that made it all the more special for Carr.

He placed his hand over the top of hers and squeezed. Moving their fists together up and down his long erection, he showed her what to do.

"Don't be shy, baby. You won't hurt it. Stroke him firm and long. Squeeze it when you get near the top." Carr whispered his instructions. When she got the rhythm, he let go of her hand and let her take over.

Jessica's little hand worked back and forth and Carr's body shook with pleasure. She caught on quickly and he couldn't hold back the moan this time. She picked up speed and so did his breathing until he was panting and rocking his hips into her palm.

He groaned when she stopped and let go of his hard, angry cock.

"No more of that. You are getting all the fun and I want to feel you inside me." Jessica moved higher and sank down on his throbbing erection. She slowly took him inside her bit by bit, her warm, wet heat engulfing him, making him moan. He was desperate to push all the way in, but knew he had to let her set the pace or he might hurt her. It was slowgoing and torturous.

When she finally sank to the hilt, Carr started to pump his hips up and down. Jessica was an amazing sight, riding his cock, her head thrown back and her small breasts bouncing. He reached up to cup them in his hands and pinched the nipples. They pebbled under his touch and he stared, fascinated.

Jessica leaned down until one of her breasts dangled over his mouth. He took the invitation and sucked her pink nipple into his mouth, suckling. Carr could tell she liked it when she moaned and drove her hips down harder on his cock.

"That is a sight I do not mind waking to." Baen's deep voice was gruff with sleep and arousal. Carr let go of Jessica's nipple and she sat up as Baen moved closer.

He knelt on the bed and took his cock in hand. "Take me in your mouth, little one. I want to feel your lips around my cock."

Jessica didn't need to be told twice. She leaned over and engulfed Baen's throbbing length in her mouth. He was too big for her to take all of him, but she used her hand to compensate and worked Baen's cock between the two.

Carr moaned at the sight and felt his arousal shoot higher. He grabbed onto Jessica's hips and started to slam her down onto his cock.

"Oh, shit, Carr. She likes what you are doing. She just tried to suck my cock straight off." Baen was moaning and pumping his cock into Jessica's mouth as she continued to ride Carr, bouncing and jostling. He was so close to coming that his grip tightened on her hips and he gritted his teeth. He didn't want to come before she did.

Baen soon roared his release and Carr watched in wonder as Jessica swallowed his load and licked him clean. Carr then turned her attention back to him as he drove his hips harder and faster into her waiting heat.

Jessica's pussy clamped down on him and she squealed her orgasm as her whole body shook above him. Carr quickly rolled them and, removing his cock from her pussy, shot his seed onto the sheet below. He groaned as he pumped his cock in his fist until he was fully spent.

Carr pulled Jessica to him and kissed her lips, showing her with his mouth just how much she meant to him. He couldn't wait for a time when he could finish without pulling from her pussy, but understood that Baen's need for an heir came first.

He knew that Baen wouldn't care who the father was and would accept any child as his own and the heir, but they were the first triad in royal history and Carr didn't want anyone challenging his sons or daughters for the throne because of their bloodline.

Marak was advanced in its thinking in some ways and still so archaic in others. Carr just didn't want to cause his family trouble later when it could be prevented now. So for now he would pull out, and once the queen was pregnant he could have his pleasures.

Carr moved off the bed and started to clean up. They changed the sheets themselves, not wanting to wake the servants, and then all jumped back into bed. He curled up with his lovers in his arms and smiled to himself. Their adventure was just starting and he couldn't wait to see what the future would hold.

* * * *

Carr woke the next morning to a banging on the chamber door. Wrapping himself in a robe, he went to growl at the person interrupting his lovers' sleep. Luckily neither of them had been disturbed by the constant knocking yet. All three had stayed up late making love and exploring each other's bodies. They had never made it down to the wedding feast and ended up calling for food to be brought to them. They weren't ready to share their new wife with anyone yet.

Jessica was just as insatiable as they were. If it wasn't Baen or him waking the others up, it was Jessica. She had even goaded them into making love to her on more than one occasion throughout the night. Baen had worried that they were a pair of horny bastards and she wouldn't be able to keep up, but it was turning out to be the opposite. If things went on like last night, they wouldn't be able to keep up with her.

Carr pulled the door open and slipped into the hall. It was one of the younger soldiers. Carr snapped at him to see what he wanted.

"Sorry to disturb you, my lord. But some of King Balfour's men have been seen crossing the border. They are a full garrison, riding heavily armed and heading this way." The man wore a worried expression on his young face, but Carr didn't have the time to soothe his fears. He would have a lot more to worry over before the day was out.

"I'll wake the King. Tell Athdar to have the men prepare for battle. We ride out in one hour." Carr didn't wait for the man's reply. He turned on his heel and went back into the chamber. He would need to hurry. Although he trusted his second-in-command, Athdar, to prepare the men, he always checked them over. You could never be too prepared when heading out to war.

Jessica was sitting up in the bed, all sleepy eyed and bedraggled. By the spirits, she was beautiful and all he wanted was to fall back in bed with her and make love to her again. Unfortunately he couldn't and he was cursing Balfour's timing. Why would he decide to attack now, the day after their wedding?

That was probably why. He must have thought he could catch them unprepared. Baen and Carr always kept their armies battle-ready. They weren't going to get caught with their pants down, not if Carr had anything to do with it.

"What's going on? Why the solemn look?" Jessica was already in tune with his feelings and Carr's heart melted all the more. They couldn't have found a more perfect woman to rule at their side and warm their bed than her. She was kind and caring and so intelligent. She was a force to be reckoned with when she put her mind to something. He hadn't known her all that long, but he couldn't wait to grow old with her and see her belly swell with their child.

But first he had to get rid of the pesky Balfour. Hopefully for the last time.

"We need to wake Baen up, baby. There's a situation we have to take care of before we can continue our honeymoon."

"I'm awake. What's the situation?" Baen popped his head up and peered at him over the top of the blankets. He was so damned cute with his hair all messed and a three-day growth. That's if a seven-foot warrior King could be called cute. Carr sighed. He had to get his head out of his ass before Balfour made it to the castle and they were all dead.

"Balfour's men have been spotted crossing the border and heading this way. I have sent for the men to be readied. We must leave at once and squash this, before they reach the castle."

"I'm certainly awake now. Have the guards doubled and the people brought inside. Then have the castle locked up. No one leaves or enters whilst we are gone." Baen was getting dressed, as he threw out orders left and right. His squire had entered with his battle armor and was helping him dress.

"What can I do?" Jessica had put on a robe and stood next to the bed looking lost. He knew she must be scared, but wasn't sure on how to soothe her. He had grown up in a world filled with fighting, but he had never had to worry about the women that were left behind.

"There is nothing you can do, baby. Why don't you go and find Fenella. She will be able to tell you what you can do around the castle to help. The people will be frightened and they will need to see their queen and be reassured."

"Oh, OK, um, well." Jessica stumbled over her words.

"All you need to do is make sure you stay safe. I will miss you. Now give me a kiss and then go and get dressed." Carr pulled Jessica into his arms and devoured her lips. He wanted to put all his feelings into that one kiss. He didn't want it to be a good-bye. He was a good warrior and had no intentions of dying out on the battlefield, not to Balfour, but things happened and he didn't want to go to his grave without this.

"Now go and see Baen. We have to go, but it shouldn't take too long."

"How can you say that? You are going to battle and you are acting like it's a normal occurrence and that you'll be home by dinner." Jessica was beautiful when she was riled. Glaring up at him, with her little hands on her hips.

"It is only a nuisance, baby. Nothing to worry over. Balfour and his men are poorly trained and are no match for my army. We will rip through their defenses and he will go home crying, like he always does."

"Carr, you shouldn't underestimate your enemy. It is when you are comfortable and arrogant enough to think nothing will defeat you that you will lose. Don't take this lightly. I will not be made a widow a day after my wedding."

"You are correct, my love. But I am never one to let down my defenses or underestimate my opponent. I will return to you and make sure Baen returns to you as well." Carr kissed her one last time and then ushered her over to Baen. They didn't have much time left and they needed to go.

He watched them say their good-byes as he finished putting on his armor and heard Baen say something about not letting his sister talk her into mischief. He smiled to himself and then strode from the room. He had orders to give and an army to prepare. It was going to be a long day.

Carr sighed. He was getting too old for this. He used to love the fighting and the life of a warrior, but now he just wanted peace. He wanted to sit around the fire and watch his husband and wife make love. He wanted to have children and watch them grow and teach them about life and about love.

That was not to be, though. Not until they either made peace with Balfour or they killed him. He hoped for the latter. Only problem was, when you cut off one evil head another rose in its place. It seemed they would always be at war. Carr had other things to occupy his time now and just wanted this over with, so he could get back to loving his family. He had waited years for Baen to marry him and he wasn't about to let some greedy, fat, pompous ass destroy his peace.

Carr reached the armory and took in the organized chaos. His men were all rushing to get ready and followed his orders with timed precision. Carr moved over to the weapons and pulled his sword from the shelf. There was nothing fancy about his steel sword. It had no jewels or markings, and the handle was plain, but it fit his grip to perfection. The blade was sharp and strong and had cut through many an enemy.

His sword was the one thing he had left of his father, who had died in battle when he was a child. His mother had died of consumption a few years later and he missed them both terribly. After their death he had been raised alongside the king, who was only a prince then, and had called Baen's parents family.

Carr put the sword back in its leather sheath after checking it over and moved out of the armory to find Athdar and get a report of the progress. His squire would be preparing his steed, so that was one less thing to worry about.

Damned Balfour again with his poor timing.

Chapter Ten

It had been over a week since the men had left for battle and Jessica had heard hardly a word. Every so often a soldier would return from the battlefield with orders for more supplies or to give an update on progress, but it was always the same. The battle raged on, and though they were driving Balfour's army further and further back there was no sign of retreat.

All she could do was sit and wait and hope that her men returned to her. Fenella was a huge comfort, but she could do only so much to assuage Jessica's fears. An easy battle, Carr had said. If this were easy she would hate to see hard.

Jessica had tried everything to keep herself occupied. She had strolled through the market and talked with its people and helped them where she could. She had tidied her chambers, much to the servant's horror. She had read stories to the children that lived in the castle and she had helped the cook plan weekly menus. She had even tried to go over the notes she had on the gateways to the other realms, but nothing had worked.

Now she was sitting in the great hall with Fenella and Elvinia, trying to learn needlepoint. She just couldn't get the hang of it and it was so boring. Jessica was going out of her mind. She put down her work and started to pace. She didn't care if Fenella thought every good wife sat by the fire and sewed. She couldn't do it anymore.

She missed her men and was worried sick. She wanted to see their faces again. She wanted to watch their big forms as they stomped down the corridor. Mostly she wanted to hold them in her arms, to watch their faces as they made love.

"Sit down, Jessica. Your pacing is making me dizzy." Elvinia's voice cut through her thoughts.

"Then stop watching me. I can't just sit and wait. It's driving me crazy. I want to pull my hair out." Jessica turned to Fenella. "How can you sit here and stay so calm, time after time?"

"It's not easy, my dear. I'd like to say it gets easier, but I would be lying. It is a heavy burden for the people left behind, but it's a woman's place to keep the home fires burning."

"Jeez, Mother. You sound so archaic. Women have just as much right to fight for their kingdom as men. How can we be so forward-thinking about some things and so behind in others" Elvinia rolled her eyes as she spoke. Fenella sent her an indulgent look. It was obviously something that they had spoken about often.

"A man would be too distracted protecting his woman, rather than focusing on the battlefield. This we have gone over and over. Besides, you are the princess. You will never be allowed to put yourself in that kind of danger." Jessica agreed with the queen mother in some aspects of her argument.

It was the same argument as the one back on her Earth. Should women be allowed on the front lines? Jessica was of the mind that, yes, women should be able to fight if that is what they want. It was their life to risk and they had just as much right to defend their country as men did. That being said, she wasn't one to join the army. She was a pacifist for the most part, but had great respect for the men and women that did defend their country.

"I need to get some air. I'm going to go for a walk along the battlements." Jessica turned and walked from the great hall. She made her way along the corridors and up the windy staircase. She had spent hours exploring the castle. Now she had so much time on her hands and finally knew her way around without getting lost.

Jessica pushed open the heavy door that led out onto the battlement. The air was cool, but there was no wind, so Jessica didn't see the point in going all the way back for her cloak. She walked along the wall and looked out toward the horizon. She ignored the soldiers on watch as she passed them, her thoughts on her men.

She wished she could see the battle from here. That way she could assure herself that they were all right. Were they still pushing back the enemy troops? How many soldiers had they lost? Were they injured? Were they hungry? Did they miss her as much as she missed them?

She sighed as she stopped at one of the arrow turrets in the castle wall and looked out. She hated this and just wanted it to be over so she could hold them in her arms. She realized in that moment that she loved them. Loved them both as equally as each other, and she wanted her family back.

She loved Baen for his gruff dominance and the way he took care of her, even when she thought she could take care of herself. She loved how proud he was of his kingdom and how he ruled it with compassion and understanding. She loved his big masculine body and the way he used it to make love to her. She also loved how he wasn't afraid to love Carr with an open passion. He was true to Carr in every way.

As for Carr, well, she loved him too. She loved his playful side and the way he could always make her and Baen smile no matter how foul their mood. For the way he protected her and Baen. She loved him for his patience and for putting himself second when Baen's duties came first. Jessica also loved his big, scarred body. The scar that ran the length of his face was a testimony to his life on the battlefield and the struggles he had to overcome. It didn't put her off.

God, she had it bad. She knew that they were getting under her skin, but she didn't realize just how much. She was going to follow them around like a lovesick puppy. She had to pull herself together before they got back. She would allow herself one day to smother them in her love and affection and then she would get back to her old self. She wasn't going to turn into one of those sappy women that wouldn't have a life of her own because she was too busy chasing after her man. No, she was stronger than that.

Who was she fooling? Her husbands would have her tied around their big scarred fingers and she would be lost. And she would love every minute of it, as long as they loved her just as fiercely.

Jessica shivered with the cold and turned to go in. The sun was starting to set on another long day and with it came the frosty chill of the night. As she started to walk along the wall and back toward the door, she thought it strange that the soldiers on lookout were missing. She had passed three on the way out and they were all gone. Maybe it was the changing of the guard. Still, it gave Jessica the creeps, so she picked up her pace and hurried along.

When she finally reached the heavy wooden door and there still was no guard inside, she was well and truly spooked. Why would they leave the battlement empty? There was a war going on. Surely they would always have people on watch. They should change the guard out on the battlement, where they could always see what was going on. She would have to talk to someone about that.

She struggled to pull the heavy door open, and when she finally got it open enough, she slipped through. What she found on the other side had her stomach rolling. The three soldiers from before were piled up, dead, with their throats slit. They lay on their backs with their eyes open and surprised looks frozen on their faces. Blood covered their bodies, and ran down onto the castle floor.

Jessica sucked in a scream and tried not to gag. She had never seen a dead body before and certainly not ones as gory as these. She had to alert the other soldiers that they had an enemy in the castle.

Looking away from the bodies, she moved to start down the winding staircase. A large form moved to block her exit and Jessica looked up into the face of the killer. He was taller than her, but not as big as her men, and had dirty-brown hair and an unshaven face. He was dressed in armor, the same as the other soldiers, but she had a feeling this man wasn't one of Carr's troops. He still held the bloody dagger in his hand and Jessica couldn't help but stare at it as the blood ran from the blade and dripped onto the floor below.

"Going somewhere, Your Majesty?" His voice was rough, like he'd smoked too many cigarettes, and his breath was foul enough to make Jessica cover her mouth with her hand.

"Please, I'm nobody. I'm just a servant who needed some air. If you let me go, I'll tell nobody that you were here." Jessica prayed he believed her and let her go, but she didn't like her chances.

"Nice try, my lady. I was at your wedding, see. So I know just who you are."

Shit. She knew it was a long shot, but she had to try.

"I have orders to take you to my lord. He wants you alive, you see. But accidents happen. Maybe we can have a little play, you and me, whilst I take you to him. He said nothin' about not being able to touch you." The vile man grabbed his crotch and rubbed himself as he stared back at her. Jessica had to fight the urge to gag again.

"That's disgusting."

Jessica felt a slap to her face and tasted blood in her mouth. It hurt like the dickens. She had never been slapped before and didn't really want to have it happen again, but she'd be damned if she let him rape her.

She decided to go meekly for now and make her move when the time was right. He still had to get her out of the castle. A castle that was filled with soldiers, which were sworn to protect her.

The man really stank, a thought that Jessica couldn't seem to let go. He grabbed her around the waist and held the knife to her throat. He shoved her forward and they started to slowly descend the winding staircase. It was slowgoing, with the blade nicking her delicate skin. He shoved and jostled her down each stair.

When they finally reached the bottom, there was still no one in sight. Where was everybody when you needed them? Her heart was pounding in her chest and she was breaking out in a cold sweat. What happened if he did manage to get her out of the castle? She would never survive it, not if he tried to lay those unwashed paws on her body.

They made their way along the corridor and through the empty great hall. He paused at the door and listened. Jessica wondered if she should scream, but decided against it. He would cut her throat for sure, and then she'd be dead. Pushing her against the wall, he held the knife to her throat as he turned and opened the door a crack. There must not have been anyone on the other side. He opened it wider and pulled her through.

Jessica moved slowly, trying to stall. She thought that if she slowed them down enough, someone would come along. She just hoped that is wasn't Fenella or Elvinia. She didn't want to put them in danger.

After they walked the length of the corridor, down another flight of stairs, and along another long corridor, they stopped at a door. Jessica was starting to panic. This was ridiculous, normally she couldn't walk through the castle without tripping over the servants or guards, but there was no one in sight.

Jessica was also lost. She had never been this far down into the belly of the castle. Baen and Carr had told her it led to the soldiers' quarters and that it was forbidden for her to explore. Normally she would have brushed off the order, but when it came to rooms filled with men, she thought it was best to be cautious.

He pulled her through the door and into a small closet room. It was dusty and the air was musty. He threw her up against the wall and air left her lungs in a gush.

"Move and I'll kill you where you stand!" His breath was hot and foul as he spat his threat in her face. Jessica nodded her head and struggled to breathe. She could feel the blood running down her neck from the small nick the knife had made.

He left her side and moved to the opposite wall. Shoving a large wooden table aside, a small wooden door was revealed. He crouched down and pulled it open. The tunnel behind it was small and long. It was dark and cobweb filled.

"Get your ass in there, wench. We still have a long way to go and I'm hungry," he told her. Surely he didn't expect her to crawl through that thing?

"Are you serious? I can't go in there." Jessica shivered at the thought. "I'm scared of small spaces. I might pass out."

"You should be more scared about what I'll do to you if you don't go in there. Now move." He waved the knife at her and when she still didn't move, he started to approach. Jessica was frozen in place. She had always hated small confined spaces. This little tunnel certainly qualified.

She let out a cry as he grabbed a handful of her hair and shoved her toward the little door. Jessica fell to her knees from the force of his push. She was going to have to go in there. She swallowed back bile and crawled toward the door. When she reached it she stopped. How the hell was she supposed to see where she was going? It was pitch black.

She started to enter the tunnel after he kicked her rear with his big muddy foot. It was hard to crawl in the long dress and she had to keep her head down so she didn't hit it on the roof. Jessica heard him enter the tunnel behind her and had to wonder how he fit. She could barely make it through and she was a lot smaller than he was.

The tunnel went darker and darker the further Jessica moved down it. There was no light at the other end to guide her, so she just slowly put one hand in front of the other. All she could hear was the sound of their breathing and the pounding of her heart. She was so desperate to reach the other side that she wanted to move faster and faster. She had to force herself to slow down. She couldn't see and one wrong move could be dangerous. She didn't know if there were drops in the floor of the tunnel or in the side. She also didn't know if the tunnel turned a corner or if it was straight the whole length.

Jessica crawled for what felt like hours. She didn't know how long she could keep on going. Her arms were exhausted and her knees scraped raw from the rough surface of the tunnel's floor.

Just when she thought she would collapse, she turned another small bend and saw a light framing another trap door. The light came from the top of the tunnel, so she would have to stand up to get out.

Jessica wasn't sure where the sudden surge of energy came from, but she picked up her pace and scrambled to the door. With a force that surprised her, she reached up and shoved open the door. Hands reached down and pulled her up and out of the tunnel.

When they let her go, Jessica frantically shook off the dress and ran her hands through her hair. Now that she was out, it felt as if bugs were crawling over her body. She didn't take the time to look around or see who had pulled her from the tunnel. She just wanted to get the things off her.

"Calm down, my lady." A deep voice cut through her hysteria.

"I can't! I can feel them crawling on me! Get them off!" she cried, tears running down her face. Big hands grabbed her arms and stilled her movements. Jessica tried to shake them off, but they held firm. She was pulled toward a big chest and large arms wrapped around her. The man was rocking and shushing her, as if she were a little child.

It wasn't long before the creepy-crawly feeling subsided and her sobs turned to feminine hiccups. She looked up into the face of the man who comforted her and was surprised at the extremely handsome features staring back at her. He was a blond, blue-eyed Adonis and she just couldn't stop staring. When he smiled at her, his whole face lit up and Jessica nearly swooned. No man should be that good-looking. Jessica hated him on the spot.

She pushed out of his arms and looked over the rest of him. He was tall but not as tall as her husbands. Slim and slightly muscled, not like her big brawny men, but worst of all there wasn't a scar on the man. His hands and face were smooth and perfect. Even his exposed arms were flawless. Not a freckle or mole in sight.

Jessica rolled her eyes at the pampered ninny and looked around. She was in the woods that surrounded the castle. She could just see it in the distance. They must have crawled all the way under the grassy fields that separated the castle from the woods in case of attack.

She moved her attentions to the group of men. There were three other men, apart from the pampered Adonis and the smelly foul man that took her. They were wearing armor, but it was different from her husband's men.

"Who are you? Are you King Balfour?" Jessica directed her question to the tall Adonis. His deep masculine laugh would normally have made her heart flutter, but now she just wanted to kick him.

"No, my lady. I'm not. Bac Domhnull at you service. I am the commander of King Balfour's armies. Once we have conquered Marak, I will have the pleasure of ruling in the King's absence."

"You will never rule Marak. My husbands will see to that." She tried to sound confident, but she failed miserably.

"Ah, but see, my little dove. I have *you* now. They will come to your rescue and I will kill them. Then Marak will be mine for the picking."

"I don't think so. You place too much value on my importance. Baen and Carr love each other. I'm just there to make the heir. They will easily find another woman to take my role." She was lying through her teeth, but she had to try. She didn't want her men to risk their lives to save her. She wanted to be rescued, just not at the sacrifice of her husbands.

"You are a poor liar. Not to worry. I will beat that out of you, when you are mine."

"I will never be yours. I would rather die."

"That just might happen, little dove." Jessica gulped at his statement. She really needed to remember that these men were her enemy and dangerous. They would kill her once her usefulness ran out. One good thing, however, was if this man wanted her, the smelly one couldn't touch her. She moved closer to Bac's side and kept her mouth shut. She would just have to go back to biding her time and hope an opportunity for escape arose.

Either way she was in a world of trouble.

* * * *

Baen moved through the camp taking stock of the supplies. Carr was counting heads to account for the losses of men. The numbers would be many, as was the way with war, but to Baen even the loss of one man was too many. Every soldier held value to him and the loss was great. Not just for him, but also for the dead soldier's family and loved ones.

Baen always made sure the families of the dead were taken care of. Nobody went without in his kingdom. What was wealth if your people went hungry? No, his father had taught him that a king without people was no king at all. Whether it was keeping them safe from the enemy, like now, or making sure they had a roof over their head and food in their belly.

He finished counting the supplies and turned to his squire. They were going to need to send back for more. Their food stocks were low and the battle wasn't likely to end soon. King Balfour was determined this time and had thrown everything at them. His men were well trained, thanks to Carr, and so they had managed to force them back, but Balfour wasn't giving up.

Much more of this and he would be calling for the dragons. He hated to use them in a fight. They were strong and proud creatures and Baen hated to take advantage of the trust they had placed in him. Using the dragons was a last resort, especially when they could get injured or worse. No one else had dragons and he liked to fight fair, but he also wasn't going to lose when he had the advantage.

Baen turned his thoughts to his lovely bride. He felt bad to leave her so soon after their wedding, but it couldn't be helped. Damned Balfour and his constant bullshit. He just wanted to live a peaceful life with his wife and husband and raise his babies. Was that too much to ask? They had lived in relative peace for years. Why was he doing this now?

Jessica must be worried sick. Her new husbands were both off fighting and she had to stay behind. He had sent for an update on her well-being when he had the soldier do supply runs. From what he had gathered from his mother's short missives, she was well, missing them terribly, but coping.

Jessica was a strong woman. He knew she would be fine. Baen didn't quite realize just how much he would miss her though. He and Carr talked about her whenever they had a free moment together, and it was easy to see that they both had fallen for her and fallen hard. She completed them in a way they never thought possible. As soon as this battle was over, they would rush back to her side and start their life together and hopefully it would be a long while before they had to leave it again.

Baen shook himself out of his daydreaming when he noticed a soldier approaching from the direction of the castle. He was riding hard, his horse at a full gallop. What could be so urgent to warrant the fast pace? Jessica! His stomach dropped as he bellowed for Carr. He raced to meet the soldier and get his report. His heart was pounding and he was sick with worry for his family.

"Tell me!" he bellowed, not even giving the man a chance to dismount the labored horse.

"It's the queen, Sire. She is missing. They have searched the entire castle, but she is gone." The man stumbled over his words as he rushed to tell him.

"What do you mean she is missing? She was to be guarded at all times, never to be left alone." Baen could feel a vein throbbing on his forehead. It was going to blow if he didn't calm down.

"We have found three dead guards and a trapdoor in a storage closet that leads outside the castle walls. Sire, she was taken."

"Who was taken?" Carr asked, as he reached their side.

"Jessica is missing. They have her, Carr. When I find her, she better be alive and not have a single scratch on her or I'm going to take great pleasure in torturing the bastards that took her." Baen strode to his tent and called for his horse, Carr hot on his heels.

"I'm coming with you."

"No, you need to stay here and finish this battle. Which I'm starting to suspect was just a decoy." Baen pulled on his heavy mantle and strapped his sword to his side, then left the tent again. His steps were long and determined.

"She is my wife too, Baen. I'm coming with you. Athdar is more than capable of looking after things here." Carr was persistent, as he too strapped his sword on and approached his horse.

"Fine, you're right. We will head for the castle and find the exit to this tunnel and track them from there. I'll have someone send up the dragons to spot her from the sky. They couldn't have made it too far."

"We will find her, Baen."

"I know. Carr, I love her. I can't lose her now. I can't lose either of you." Baen reached out and grabbed a handful of Carr's overshirt in his fist. He pulled Carr toward him and planted a strong kiss to his lips. It was swift but full of meaning. He would kiss him properly once they had their wife safe and back by their side.

"I love her too, Baen. And I love you. You two are my life and it has no meaning without you in it." Carr straightened when he let go of his top.

"Let's ride out then and find our woman." Baen kicked his horse into a gallop and heard Carr following behind. When they found Jessica, he was going to take her back home and never let her leave his sight again. She would be lucky if he let her leave the bedchamber. God, he hoped she was all right and they were treating her well. It was going to be a painful death if they weren't.

Chapter Eleven

Jessica trudged along behind Bac, her hands tied together with rope. It was slowgoing and she still hadn't recovered from crawling through the tunnel. Her legs burnt and she was puffing for breath. Not to mention she was covered from head to toe in dirt and sweat. She felt rotten and just wanted to curl in a ball and sleep for a week.

Bac pulled on the rope and Jessica stumbled. She managed to catch herself before she face-planted into the dirt, but it jarred her already tired and sore legs, and the rope was rubbing her wrists raw.

"Please, I need to stop. I can't go on any further." Jessica wasn't below begging. Besides, it might slow them down even more.

"No, we have to hurry. They would have discovered you missing by now and I want to be far from the castle before they catch up with us." Bac pulled on the ropes once more and this time Jessica did fall. She landed on her knees and elbows and cried out as the pain shot through her body.

"I cannot believe Baen and Carr would choose such a weak woman. Maybe I will have to rethink keeping you." Bac looked down at her when she rolled onto her back and refused to move. She would have taken exception to his comment, if she had the strength to do more than lie there. Not the part about keeping her, but the part about her being weak.

"Don't you have horses? Not only would it have been faster, but also then I wouldn't have to walk. Can't King Balfour afford to give his commander a horse?" She was goading him, but she didn't care.

"We have horses, wench. They would have been too noisy to bring and we would have been discovered. Now get moving."

"I can't. Just leave me here and make your escape." She could see Bac clench his jaw as he got angrier with her. She needed to stop saying things that made him mad before he took his anger out on her.

When she still refused to move—and it wasn't because she was being difficult, it was just that she was so damned tired—Bac grabbed her by the front of her dress and hauled her to her feet. He then bent down and flung her over his shoulder. Her head and arms dangled down near his ass and he held her behind her knees.

"Let's get moving. I want to be clear of these woods by sunset." Bac wasn't talking to her, but to the men. She lay slumped over his shoulder and tried to breathe. It was a really uncomfortable position, and as he moved her belly bounced on his shoulder.

"Put me down. I'm going to lose my lunch all down your back," she told him.

"Do that and you will regret the consequences." He gave her a hard swat to her rear. It pissed her off. She leant forward and retaliated by sinking her teeth into the back of his hard thigh. It was difficult to get a good chunk because his thighs were so solid and smooth. There was nothing to grab onto. It made him laugh and swat her behind once more.

"If Balfour wanted to use me to get to the king, why did he send you?" Jessica asked from her upside down position.

"You still think that Balfour is the mastermind behind all this, don't you?" Bac gave a chuckle. "This whole plan was mine. The battle, taking you, everything. Balfour is too old and stupid. He wants to sit in his castle with his ugly wife. I'm the one who takes care of everything. I'm the one who rules his kingdom, whilst he feeds his fat belly and drinks himself stupid."

"Then why do you need Marak? Why not just keep ruling Barak?"

"Because, my little dove, Marak if far richer. The lands are more prosperous and Marak has a clean water supply. Yet King Baen doesn't use the land to the best of its potential."

"You think you can rule it better?" Jessica couldn't keep the sarcasm out of her voice, but the arrogant man didn't even seem to notice.

"Of course! When I am on the throne, the people will be put to work, mining and farming the land, and the taxes will need to rise. I will give Balfour some of the profit to keep him under control, whilst I raise an army big enough to conquer all the surrounding kingdoms. They will all bow down to the one true king. I will be ruler of Earth and the most powerful man that ever lived." Great, a man who wanted to take over the Earth had kidnapped her.

Jessica found that somewhat amusing. People wrote stories all the time about crazy men who wanted to conquer the world. It was a ridiculous idea, in her Earth and this one.

"I almost had my plan well under control, when I had Baen's dear little sister poisoned. Her death was going to send the kingdom into mourning, making them an easy target ripe for the picking. I still don't know how the little bitch lived, but I'll find out and when I do..."

Jessica fell silent and zoned out his words. She didn't want to hear anymore of Bac's idea on taking over the planet. She was shocked that it was Bac that had poisoned Elvinia. She wasn't sure why she was surprised, he was the enemy. She knew he could never find out about her ability or he would use it against her. Luckily no one but Baen, Carr, and their family knew.

The further they moved on, the worse Jessica started to feel. Her stomach was hurting and she was getting a headache from hanging upside down for too long. If they didn't reach the end of the wood soon, she really was going to lose her lunch down his back.

The men walked on for hours, with Jessica flung over Bac's shoulder like a sack of potatoes. She fought back a groan, her misery complete. She felt like dying. The constant pain was overwhelming. Jessica lay there limply and tried to stay conscious. When she couldn't hold the agony in anymore, she groaned aloud.

Bac halted and slowly let her slide down his body. When her feet hit the ground, she slumped and would have fallen if it weren't for Bac still holding her.

"What is wrong with you, woman?" Jessica couldn't answer. She rested her head on his chest and moaned. He swung her up into his arms and carried her over to a small patch of grass. Gently laying her down, Bac prodded at her stomach, making her moan louder from the pain.

"Please, no more. Just let me die." Jessica wrapped her arms around her middle and rolled into a ball. She closed her eyes and tried to shut out the people around her. Bac was having none of that.

"You are weak. I told you, you were a weak woman and now you have gone and injured yourself. I won't have it. It is slowing us down. You will get better at once." Jessica would have rolled her eyes if she had the strength. He was starting to sound like a spoilt little boy, not the flirty confident kidnapper that he was when she first came out of the tunnel.

"Let's kill her now and dump the body. Then we can wait for the bastards to come for her and ambush them, when they are mourning their loss." The husky voice of the smelly man that took her cut through her pain.

"That's not a bad idea, boss. She is dead weight anyway and has no further use." Jessica didn't know who said that, but she didn't like the direction this conversation was taking.

"No, not yet. We may still need her," Bac spat out. He turned and stood to face his men. "We need to get the horses. We aren't far from where we left them. You two go and bring them back. We will wait here. Be quick about it."

"I still think we should kill her." This came from the smelly guy.

"You're such a bloodthirsty bastard, aren't you. Go get the fucking horses or it will be you lying there dead." Bac turned his attention away from the men and crouched down over her. She was on her side facing him and when she opened her eyes a crack, Jessica noticed the dagger strapped to his thigh. It was a fancy jeweled thing, but if she could get her hands on it, she would be able to do some damage and hopefully escape. They were two men down now. It was the best chance she was going to get.

"You better yet?" Bac asked. He reached over to prod her tummy once more. Jessica bit back a groan and lay as still as possible. She wanted to take him by surprise.

Jessica waited for Bac to relax and think she was passed out. He remained crouched over her, but wasn't paying attention to her. Something in the distance had caught his notice.

She took a deep breath and felt her body tingle with anticipation. This was it. She needed to rally her courage and her strength and just go for it. She opened her eyes slightly and looked at Bac. He still was watching something in the bushes.

Jessica opened her eyes wide and with a rebellious yell that would make any warrior proud. She sat up and grabbed the dagger from its sheath in one move. Without slowing her movements or taking the time to think it over, she thrust the dagger up and into Bac's chest.

She felt the flesh give way as the blade pierced his skin and slipped into his body. Jessica let go of the dagger and shuffled herself away from Bac. He grabbed at the dagger, a look of shock and surprise on his handsome face. Blood ran from the wound and down his body in gushes.

She tried not to look, but was unable to look away. Swallowing back bile, she rolled over and got to her feet. She had to lean against a tree for support, but was able to stand.

Bac was cursing and screaming, unable to understand how a woman had gotten the better of him. Jessica watched as surprise turned to anger. He pulled the dagger from his chest, with a pain-filled groan, and stood. Shit, he was coming toward her, holding the bloody dagger in his hand. Blood still ran from the wound as he got closer and closer to her position.

"You can't kill me, bitch. I'm too strong. You could have ruled at my side, but instead you have chosen death." Bac raised the dagger high above his head and Jessica panicked. She closed her eyes and raised her arms to ward off the dagger's descent, but it never came.

She opened one eye to see that Bac had an arrow piercing his throat. The head of the arrow stuck out just enough for her to recognize it for what it was. When he slumped to the ground dead, Jessica squealed. She looked over to see Baen and Carr still mounted on their stallions. Carr still held the bow that had fired the arrow.

Jessica sighed in relief at the sight of her husbands. She looked down at Bac and her stomach rolled at the gory sight. She hurried behind the nearest tree and promptly threw up.

* * * *

Baen and Carr had ridden up just in time to see Jessica drive the dagger into Bac's side. Carr's heart had stopped in that moment and it wasn't until Bac had pulled the dagger from his body and raised it to stab Jessica that he was thrown into action and grabbed his bow. The arrow had pierced Bac's neck seconds before the knife's descent.

He passed his bow to one of the soldiers and dismounted as Jessica ran for the bushes. He should have expected as much. She was a delicate little thing and the sight of all that blood would send any lady into hysteria.

When she had finished vomiting and wiped her mouth, Baen and Carr pulled her into their arms. Carr was ready to comfort her while she cried and tell her that she would never have to go through an ordeal like that again.

"You took your bloody time. A second later and I could have been dead. What took you so long?" Carr was taken aback by her demanding, forceful tone. Jessica stood with her hands on her small hips, ready to do battle. Where was the weeping and hysteria? Jessica looked mad enough to spit. If looks could kill, Baen and Carr would be roasted.

"We had a little trouble finding the end to the tunnel. In the end my squire had to crawl through it and raise the alert from the other side." Baen pulled her back into his arms. She pushed him away again and held her arms out defensively.

"Stay away. I smell and I'm covered in sweat and dirt and God knows what else. I need a bath and a stiff drink. I've had a trying day." Jessica did look a fright, but to him she still was the most beautiful creature to walk the Earth. They had nearly lost her and it was going to take him a long time to recover, if ever. She didn't seem too fazed by the whole ordeal.

Baen hugged her to him and smiled down at her. Carr moved in again behind her and buried his face in her neck. He needed to hold her every bit as much as Baen. Not only to reassure himself that she was alive and well, but because he loved her with everything in him and more.

"I don't care what state you're in. We nearly lost you today. It is going to take me a very long time before I let you out of my sight again. So get used to me and most likely Carr pinned to your side." Baen's voice was gruff and filled with emotion. If Carr didn't know better he thought Baen was going to cry.

"Yes, baby. I need to know you are safe too. I will be having nightmares about today for a long time," Carr added. "When I saw Bac standing over you with his dagger raised, my heart just about stopped."

"Well, I had things well in hand. I had a plan." Jessica was such a stubborn little thing. He'd bet that she'd never admit that she needed help.

"What was your plan, baby?" Carr asked her, as they made their way back toward the horses.

"I was going to do a fancy drop-and-roll move to get out of his way. I was just waiting for the right time to make my move."

"Was that going to happen before or after he stabbed you?" Baen was smiling, as he put the question to her.

"Funny. Really funny. What happened to the other two men and the two men that were sent for the horses?"

Carr smiled at her change of subject. "You mean the two dead men over there?" he pointed to where the two bodies still lay where they fell. "I sent men after the other two. They will not be a problem for long."

They reached the horses and Carr watched as Baen mounted his stallion. He gently lifted Jessica, passed her up to Baen and watched her settle on his lap. He wanted her to ride with him, but he understood Baen's need to hold her too. He would get his chance to smother and pamper her after her long trying day later.

Carr sighed. He moved to mount his own stallion and then looked over at his lover's. Jessica had already curled into Baen's big chest and gone to sleep. His heart did a somersault at the sight. Both his lovers were safe and well. He couldn't wait to get back to the comforts of the castle. It had been weeks since he had slept in a soft bed next to his family.

Baen nudged his horse into a gentle canter, with Carr riding along beside him. The guards moved into formation around them and they all headed back toward the castle. They would leave the bodies there for the wild animals to take care of. It was a warning to anyone else that tried to hurt their family.

Normally Baen let the opposing side bury their dead, but Carr could see he wasn't in the mood to play nice. Bac and his men had tried to harm their wife. They would get no mercy and no proper burial.

"When we reach the castle, send word to Balfour that his plan was thwarted and his commander is dead. If he leaves quietly and backs down, he may retrieve his dead and live to see another day." Baen's voice was hard and mirrored the anger that Carr felt.

"I'll send Athdar. He will see that the message is received loud and clear." Carr suspected that Balfour would go quietly. With Bac dead and their forces dwindling, he would only be risking his own throne by staying.

Carr knew Baen didn't want the responsibility of another kingdom. He was happy to let Balfour rule Barak, as long as he left Marak in peace. He wasn't a greedy man and he wasn't after power. He just wanted his kingdom to be safe and prosperous.

"Good, we all need rest and a good meal. Then I think we need to teach our little queen who the head of this family is."

"Yes, Jessica is," Carr said and Baen let out a laugh. Jessica shifted but didn't wake up.

"She had a fire in her eyes when she told us off for being late." Baen said, smiling. "Our little woman is full of spirit. She will keep us on our toes."

"I agree. It will take the both of us to keep her in line. Spirits help us, if she ever learns just how much she has us wrapped around her little finger."

"Do you think she has given up on the idea of going home? If she decides she wants to, I don't think I can give her up. I love her too damned much." Carr heard the worry in Baen's voice. He, too, was worried that she wanted to leave. She still hadn't given up her search to find a way home and that made them insecure.

"All we can do is wait and see, and try to show her that by our side and in our bed is where she belongs. But I can see the love in her eyes. I really feel she will want to stay," Carr said.

"Even if she has men trying to kill her? There will always be someone trying to take control of our kingdom and putting her life at risk "

"I hear you, my love. But you know we will always put her safety first. The bastard Bac got lucky. We will never be that lax again. Jessica will have no reason to fear for her life or the lives of her babies. You are just feeling jittery because we almost lost her."

"I know you are right. It will take a while to get over this scare and return to normal."

They broke out of the woods and rode into the grassy patch that separated the castle from the woods. They were almost home and, with every step closer, Carr felt the tension leave his body.

Chapter Twelve

Baen woke curled around Jessica with his arm stretched out so his hand rested on Carr's waist. They had all fallen into bed late last night after they had bathed and eaten. Baen and Carr had checked Jessica from head to toe for injuries. Her ribs and stomach were still tender from spending so much time over Bac's shoulder, but they would heal. He had sent for the healer Elsbeth to patch up the nick to her neck caused by the dagger.

He had paced back and forth the entire time, cursing the bastard that had dared to cause his little wife pain. Every time she so much as winced as Elsbeth tended to her, Baen grew more and more agitated. Carr had attempted to calm him down, reminding him that it was over and that she was safe and back in their arms, but it was no use. He had worked himself up and it wasn't until Elsbeth had finished and left that Jessica was able to soothe the raging anger inside himself.

Spirits, he loved her and he had almost lost her. His enemy had gotten the better of him and that was unacceptable. He wished he could go back and kill Bac all over again or at least torture him for a while.

Baen lifted up and placed his hand under his head. He looked down at his sleeping wife and husband. They were his world. Jessica looked so little and fragile in her sleep, but Baen knew better. She was a strong woman, full of fire, and a match for Carr and himself in every way. Carr was right when he said she had them wrapped around her little finger. He would give her anything she wanted.

He sighed and looked toward his other lover. Carr had a peacefulness to him when he was asleep. His face softened and the hard lines smoothed out. His scar looked less threatening and he almost looked boyish. Not that he would ever say that to Carr. His lover would take offense at him saying something like that.

"Couldn't sleep?" Jessica asked. He looked down at her and then leant down to place a gentle kiss upon her lips. She had a big bruise on her cheek from where one of Bac's men had hit her. He clenched his jaw and held back the swearword that threatened to escape.

"No, I'm awake now and ready to show you just how much I've missed you." Baen continued to kiss her, running his hand along her side and up to tangle in her hair.

"Baen, I missed you and Carr so much. When Bac took me, I thought…well, I thought I wouldn't get the chance to tell you how much I love you." Jessica nipped at his lips and he breathed in her scent. It was fresh like the lemon soap she had used last night and a smell that was distinctly Jessica.

"You are so beautiful, my little queen. I love you too. I was going crazy when I thought I might never see you again. You light up my life, little one, and bring brightness and joy to a dark, battle-filled world. I'm never giving you up. You are mine now, mine and Carr's."

"I'm not going anywhere. I love you both too much to ever leave you."

"Good, because we would never let you. Now roll over and tell me how much you love me." Carr pulled her from his arms and took her mouth in a passionate kiss. Baen felt his cock getting hard at the sight of his lovers kissing.

"I do love you, Carr. So much. You are my big warrior and I love every solid inch of you." Jessica untangled herself from Carr's arms and sat up to pull her nightgown over her head.

When she lay down again, she was naked as the day she was born. He stared at her body and his cock hardened more. He was desperate to make love to her, but she was injured and he didn't want to hurt her more. Baen moved to leave the bed and remove himself from the tempting sight.

"Where do you think you're going?" Jessica asked. She grabbed his arm and pulled him back to her.

"You are injured, little one. Your stomach is black and blue. I don't want to hurt you, but if you stay lying there like that, I don't think I'll be able to help myself."

"Baen is right, baby. You must be sore," Carr added.

"I'm fine. I may be small, but compared to you everyone is. I'm not going to break, and I need my husbands to make love to me. To show me how much they care and to wipe away the bad memories of yesterday."

"You are a sly little thing aren't you?" Carr smiled down at her, and then stared to remove his breeches. They had both gone to bed wearing their pants not wanting to upset Jessica with their manly urges. It seemed they had little to worry about.

"Well, I hope it's working. Hurry up and get naked. I need my lovers to fuck me. I want to feel your hard cocks inside me."

Baen ripped off his breeches as Carr moved back to lie at Jessica's side. He ran a hand along her stomach and up to cup one of her firm breasts. Baen watched as Carr kissed her, their tongues tangling. When he had watched enough, he moved closer and reached out to take Carr's long erection in his fist. He squeezed it and jerked it, as Carr made love to Jessica's mouth. He didn't stop until Carr was panting for breath, his cock hard and angry in Baen's hand.

He let go of Carr and moved his attention to Jessica. He ran a hand over her torso and cupped her free breast with his hand. Tweaking her nipple between his thumb and finger, he played with the bud until it was hard and pebbled. Baen moved his hand down her body to tangle in her curls. Her pussy was damp and her little clit poked out from beneath its hood.

Moving down her body, he spread her thighs wide. Making a spot for himself between her legs, he dove in. Running his tongue from her bottom to her clit, Baen moaned when her flavor burst on his tongue.

He loved her unique taste and could stay down there all day, licking and teasing her pussy with his tongue.

Baen slipped one long finger inside her tight channel and curled his finger. She shifted and moaned on the bed under him and spread her legs wider in invitation.

"Fuck, that's so hot. You have a gorgeous pussy, baby. When Baen is finished, I want a taste. But first…" Carr moved away from Jessica and pushed at Baen's hips. He rolled to the side to give Carr access to his cock. Carr didn't mess around engulfing his entire length into the hot cavern of his mouth.

"Now that is hot." Jessica's voice was breathy with arousal. "Bring your cock up here, Carr, and let me have a taste."

Baen lifted his head to say, "Good plan, little one. I think our little wife is as adventurous in bed as we are, Carr." Baen went back to licking Jessica's sweet pussy as Carr moved into position. His cock jerked when he felt the vibrations of Carr's moan. Jessica must have done something he liked because Carr was going to suck his cock straight off, he was working at it so hard.

Baen added another finger to her tight channel, stretching her and preparing her for his big cock. He started to move his fingers in and out quicker and harder as she humped her hips up at him. Baen didn't stop until she was crying out her orgasm, her whole body shaking with the intensity.

He lifted his head and Carr moved from his cock.

"Get the grease, Carr. I want you in my ass as I fuck our little wife." Baen smiled at the look on Carr's face. It was rare indeed, when he let Carr fuck him, but he wanted to feel both his lovers at the same time, he needed to feel his lovers at the same time. Maybe then he could calm down and things could return to normal.

"Are you sure, Baen? I don't have to, if you don't want." Carr's voice was hesitant and he didn't like it.

"I wouldn't have said it if I didn't mean it. Now get the grease and start preparing me for your cock." Baen moved up Jessica's body and lifted her legs over his arms. It spread her wide and left nothing unavailable to his touch.

He leant down and kissed her, sucking on her tongue and nipping at her lips. He was getting desperate to be inside her, to show her through his actions just how much he loved her. If it took the rest of his days, he was going to make sure she knew just how much he needed her and by letting Carr take his ass, he was doing the same thing. They were his lovers and his life, now and forever.

* * * *

Jessica sucked on Baen's tongue and tasted her own juices on his lips. He was a passionate man and Jessica hoped that she could keep up. She was turned on by the thought of Baen fucking her while Carr fucked him, and she felt her pussy throb and demand attention, despite the fact that she had just had an orgasm.

Her men had turned her into a horny, crazed wanton, but she didn't care. She loved everything they had taught her about her body and theirs and couldn't wait to learn what else they had in their sexual repertoire.

Baen broke the kiss and moved to place his cock at her entrance. He slowly pushed forward and parted her lips with his massive girth. He entered her with aggravating slowness, and because of the position he held her in she was powerless to do anything about it. When he finally was impaled to the hilt, he stopped and bent down to rest his head in his hand. He acted like he had all the time in the world, as opposed to the fact he was balls deep in her pussy and she was horny as hell.

"You know once you have healed properly, I'm going to spank your ass good." Baen smiled down at her. Her heart did a flip at his words, but her pussy clenched around his length. There was no hiding the fact that the idea turned her on.

"Um, why?" she asked, and her pussy clenched again at his cheeky smile.

"By going out on the battlements, you put your life in danger and disobeyed the one rule I gave you whilst we were gone. You were not to go anywhere without a full escort. That included anywhere inside the castle."

"I thought I would be safe inside the castle. Otherwise I would have stayed with your mother." It wasn't really fair. She hadn't disobeyed him deliberately.

"I see I need to assign someone to guard you whenever Carr or I can't be with you." Baen looked over his shoulder at Carr, as he returned to the bed with the grease in his palm. "What do you think, Carr?"

"It's a good idea, my love. Someone who is in charge of her safety at all times when we can't be there will give peace of mind to us both." Carr removed the lid on the jar and moved in behind Baen. Jessica couldn't see what he was doing anymore, but could guess when Baen stiffened and groaned above her.

He pushed his hip forward and then back again, slowly working his cock in and out of her tight channel. Jessica wasn't even sure he was aware of his movements, he was so focused on what was going on behind him.

"Whatever you're doing back there, you need to hurry. I can't take much more." She was desperate for Baen to start moving inside her properly, not these small teasing movements that he was doing now.

"Patience, baby. I need to prepare Baen properly. He is so tight, I fear I will hurt him." Carr smiled at her over Baen shoulder. His cheeky grin was infectious and Jessica couldn't help but smile back.

"Fuck, I forgot how good this feels. Hurry up, Carr. I need to feel your cock. Jessica is squeezing me so hard, I'm not going to last much longer." Baen's voice held the desperation she was feeling.

"All right, my love. You are ready. Hold still," Carr said. Baen's long groan above her told her all she needed to know. He snapped his hip forward and it felt like his huge cock was all the way inside her stomach. His hips started to move back and forth, the pace increasing as he moved closer and closer to finishing. Jessica moaned and pushed her hips up at him, grinding her clit against him.

"Oh shit, oh fuck. It feels so fucking good. Your cock feels so big in my ass, lover, and Jessica's tight pussy is wrapped around me like silken heat." Baen moaned out his words as he continued to work his cock in her cunt and Carr's cock in his ass.

"I forgot how good your ass feels, lover. I wonder if Jessica's ass feels this good." Carr said. He was grunting and groaning behind Baen and Jessica could hear the slapping of flesh as his hips slapped onto Baen's ass checks.

"I can tell you, that she does. Her tight little hole sucks your cock straight in."

"Oh God, you two. Just shut up and fuck me already." Jessica was so close to orgasm that she could taste it. She didn't want to come again this soon, wanting the moment to last forever.

"I don't think our little baby likes dirty talk, Baen."

"Well, she will just have to get used to it. Her pussy is so tight and hot and driving me wild." Baen chuckled as he talked dirty. Jessica didn't mind dirty talk, but her husbands were getting distracted. She put a stop to his talk by leaning up and taking his mouth with her own. She sucked his bottom lip between her lips and pulled as she snapped her hips up at him and drove his cock hard into her depths.

He took the hint and drove into her hard and fast. Jessica climbed higher and higher toward orgasm. She knew it was going to be explosive as her inside tightened and her pussy clenched and relaxed on Baen's cock.

Jessica screamed as her orgasm washed over her and left her shaking and panting for breath. She tightened her arms around Baen as he continued to pound into her before yelling his completion. She felt her pussy flood with his hot jism, as her cunt shook with the aftermath of her own orgasm.

"Fuck!" Carr roared from behind Baen and they all collapsed into a pile, spent and exhausted.

"That was amazing. I love you both so much. I wish we could stay this way forever," she told them. Her heart hurt with the love she felt for them.

"I love you too, baby," Baen replied. "You are more than I could have ever wished for. "

"I too, love and adore you," Carr added. "We can stay this way forever. You're stuck with us, remember."

It was a long while before anyone moved and when they did it was only to get cleaned up before jumping back into bed together, snuggling in each other's arms and whispering nonsense. Baen had told her that Athdar had convinced Balfour it was in his best intentions to retreat and never to return. As his heart wasn't really in the fight and Bac had been the driving force behind the entire battle, he had packed up his army and scurried back to Barak. Carr had said that it was doubtful that they had seen the last of him, but it would be a while before he pulled another stunt like that.

Jessica was glad. She had missed her men and didn't really like being taken hostage either. Now they could settle into married life and get to know each other better. Jessica had plans for her men that didn't involve leaving the bed anytime soon.

She loved her husbands with a fierce possessiveness that frightened and excited her. She knew that they loved her back just as much. She wasn't going anywhere. She was still going to try and find a pattern to the gateways and maybe a way home. She would like her husbands to see her Earth too, but only for a visit. She liked the mystery of the veils and took it as a challenge to find out as much as she could about them. She would spend time with Diarmad and maybe they could figure it out together.

Here she felt accepted. Her magic still needed to be kept a secret, for protection if nothing else, but she would still use it if the need arose.

Jessica knew her place was here now, with her husbands whom she loved. She may have started her journey looking for something magical, but what she found in Baen's and Carr's arms was much, much more.

THE END

ABOUT THE AUTHOR

I live in Melbourne, Australia, with my husband, two children, and a Maltese Jack Russell who can't stop barking. I had my first idea for a story whilst working as a chef at the local pub. I have been addicted to reading since my ninth-grade teacher read us *The Outsiders* by S.E. Hinton. From then on I read anything I could get my hands on. Now, I love to read stories with a happy-ever-after ending, especially erotic romance. When I'm not running after my kids, I usually can be found cooking, reading, or writing.

For all titles by McKinlay Thomson, please visit
www.bookstrand.com/mckinlay-thomson

Siren Publishing, Inc.
www.SirenPublishing.com